The Last Pendragon

Book one in *The Last Pendragon Saga*

The
LAST
PENDRAGON

by

SARAH WOODBURY

The Last Pendragon
Copyright © 2011 by Sarah Woodbury

This is a work of fiction.

To Brynne, for the inspiration to write at all,
To Carew, for his invaluable help with plot and form,
To Gareth, for his undivided attention,
To Taran, for time,
To my parents, for history,
And to Dan, for everything else.

He who searches for enlightenment,
Shall find confusion.
He who seeks to slay another,
Shall slay himself.
He who travels to the deepest reaches of the Underworld,
Shall find heaven.
He who has lost his soul and cannot save himself,
Shall save us all.
—Taliesin, *The Black Book of Gwynedd*

Dinas Bran, North Wales, Kingdom of Gwynedd

PROLOGUE

634 AD

Dinas Bran, North Wales, Kingdom of Gwynedd

Taliesin

Water streamed in rivulets down the stone walls as I stood at the kitchen door of the castle, seeking shelter from the weather. I pushed the door open farther, the rain dripping from my hood, and confronted the weeping woman.

"Give the boy to me."

With tears pouring down her face, a match to the drops of rain on mine, Alcfrith, sister to the great King Penda of Mercia and wife of Cadwallon, the King of Gwynedd, handed me the sleeping child.

I took him and studied the face of his mother. She'd lost her husband and the boy, his father, in battle ten days before, killed far from home in Saxon lands. Although the woman did not yet know, Cadwallon had been struck down by the very man who now sought to marry her. That man would be known forever as Cadfael the Usurper. I didn't tell her the future I saw or that she would live to regret her choices. As of this moment, the boy, this child of an ancient and powerful lineage, was an orphan and my responsibility.

"Don't tell me where you're taking him," Alcfrith said. "I cannot bear to know."

"Safer that you don't," I said.

And that was that. I turned away from the woman; didn't even bother to nod at the guard who thought to block my way, just brushed past him. As old as I was, having sought a prophecy my whole life, I could no longer afford to think about anything but the one thing that mattered: *is this boy the one?*

My brotherhood had searched for him for centuries, but with each child we found, each great man we shaped, we found ourselves disappointed. Human greed, lust, an insatiable quest for power, either in them or in those who pledged to serve them, had always brought them to their knees. For hundreds of years, through the coming of the Romans who destroyed our sacred sites, and then the Saxons, whose gods were strange and barbaric, we'd charted the stars, fought the demons we could, and watched the signs, each time hoping and praying that this boy would be the one.

Would Cadwaladr? His father had ruled with a strong arm, but I'd known at Cadwallon's birth that despite a vision of great victories that would be his, he too would falter, dying too young to keep either the Saxon menace or the gods at bay. This usurper Cadfael—I found myself snorting under my breath at the thought of his rule. Gwynedd would suffer under that one, although the Council would not see it until it was far too late—and longer still until such a time as the boy in my arms could claim his birthright.

The stars had aligned for this child, more than for any other, even the great Arthur who'd protected his people for a generation. The Dragon stood menacingly in the night sky, one claw outstretched, shining down upon the Cymry—the free people of Wales. The end of one dragon's life was the beginning of another's. Would he come to land? Would he inhabit the soul of this boy and lead us to victory as we all hoped he would? In truth, even the gods didn't know for sure, and the little they told me was not enough.

Alcfrith stood in the doorway of the castle, watching me cross to the postern gate, the light spilling past her into the muddy courtyard. As I reached the gate, rain fell on the boy's head, and he stirred. I was tempted to look back.

Instead, I adjusted the boy on my shoulder. The light behind me would illumine his face and give his mother one last look at what she was losing.

I am not without pity.

1

Aberffraw, North Wales,

Kingdom of Gwynedd

655 AD

Rhiann

The smell of smoke and sweat filled the hall, mingling with the overlay of roast pig and boiled vegetables. More soldiers than usual sat at the long tables, here to celebrate their victory. The mood was subdued, however, not the wild jubilation that sometimes accompanied triumph and caused Rhiann's father to lock her in her room in case he couldn't control the men.

Today, the drinking had begun in earnest the moment the men had returned from the fight and settled into a steady rhythm Rhiann had never quite seen before. Here and there, a hand clenched a cross hung around the neck or an amulet against the powers of darkness, that should her father see, might mean death for that soldier. For a man to ask the gods for protection instead of the Christ meant he was less afraid of the King of Gwynedd than someone, or perhaps something, else. Rhiann had been afraid of her father her whole life and couldn't imagine fearing another more, not even the demons that were said to walk the night, hungering for men's souls.

Perspiration trickled down the back of Rhiann's dress, made of the finest blue wool that her father had gotten in trade from merchants on the continent. Welsh wool, while plentiful, was courser than that of sheep raised in warmer climates. The Saxon threat was enough to keep the Cymry within their own borders, but the sailors still took to the western seas, bringing in trade goods of wine, finely wrought cloth, metalwork, and pottery.

For once, Rhiann's father, King Cadfael of Gwynedd, had eaten little and drunk less. For her own preservation, Rhiann had always been sensitive to his moods and noted the exact instant his disposition changed. He shifted in his seat and rolled his shoulders, like a man preparing for a battle instead of the next course of his meal. A moment later, the big, double doors to the hall creaked open, pushed inward by two of the men who always guarded them. The rain puddled in the courtyard behind them, and Rhiann wished she were out in it instead of here—anywhere but here.

She kept her place, standing behind and to the left of her father's chair. It was her duty to tend to his needs at dinner as punishment for her refusal to marry the man he'd chosen for her. Rhiann hadn't turned the man down because he didn't love her, or she him; she knew better than to wish for that. It was a hope for mutual respect for which she was holding out. But even this seemed too much to ask for an unloved, bastard daughter. Consequently, Rhiann spent her days as a maidservant, albeit one who worked above stairs. She didn't regret her station. As the months passed, she'd come to prefer it to sharing space at the table with her father and his increasingly belligerent allies.

Silence descended on the hall as two of King Cadfael's men-at-arms entered, dragging between them a young man whose head fell so far forward that no one could see his face. He was visibly collapsed, with his arms dangling over the guards' shoulders and his feet trailing behind him. As the trio progressed along the aisle between the tables toward the king's seat, the youth seemed to recover somewhat, getting his feet under him and managing to keep up with their strides. As he came more to himself, he straightened further.

By the time he reached the dais on which Rhiann's father sat, he was using the men-at-arms as crutches on either side of him. Because he was significantly taller than they, it was even as if he was hammering them into the ground with his weight. His footsteps rang out more firmly with every stride, echoing from floor to ceiling, matching the drumming of Rhiann's heart. The closer he got to her father, the harder it became to swallow her tears. *By the souls of all the Saints, Cadwaladr, why did you come?*

Rhiann had been her father's prisoner her whole life, unable to escape his iron hand. The high, wooden palisade that circled Aberffraw had always signified prison walls to her, rather than a means to protect her from the darkness beyond. This young man had grown up on the other side of that wall. He'd not had to enter here. He'd had a choice, but had recklessly thrown that choice away and was now captive, just as she was. She felt herself dying a little inside with every step he took as he approached Cadfael.

The young man, Cadwaladr, the last of the Pendragons, fixed his eyes on those of the woman sitting beside the King. She was Alcfrith, Cadfael's wife, taken as bride after the death of Cadwaladr's father. Rhiann couldn't see her face, but from the back, the tension was a rod up her spine, and her shoulders were frozen as if in ice.

"Hello, Mother." Cadwaladr's lips were cracked and bleeding, puffy from the beating that had bruised the whole length of him. Rhiann had heard they'd close to killed him, but from the look of him now, he wasn't yet at death's door.

"Son." Alcfrith's voice was as stiff as her body.

Rhiann's father ranged back in his chair, legs crossed at the ankles to project his calm and deny the importance of the moment. "Foolish whelp. I'd thought you'd put up more of a fight, not that I regret the ease of your defeat. This will allow me to reinforce my eastern border more quickly than I'd thought. Penda will be pleased."

"You and I both know why my company was not prepared for battle today," Cadwaladr said.

Cadfael shrugged. "Your men are dead and you a shell of a man. What did you think? That the people would welcome you? That I would let you take my lands?"

"My lands," Cadwaladr said.

Rhiann's father sneered his contempt. He reached out an arm to Alcfrith and massaged the back of her neck. She didn't bend to him. If anything, the tension in her increased. "You meet your death tomorrow, as proof of your ignobility."

Cadfael waved his hand to Rhiann, signaling her to refill his cup of wine and that the interview was over. She obeyed, of course, stepping forward with her carafe. The guards tugged on Cadwaladr, but as he moved, Rhiann glanced up and met his eyes. It was only for a heartbeat, but in that space it seemed to Rhiann that they were the only ones in the room. She expected to see desperation and fear in him, or at the very least, pain. Instead, she saw understanding. She could hardly credit it. When had she ever known that?

"You're wrong, Father," Rhiann said, as the guards hauled Cadwaladr away. "Cadwaladr comes to us as a defeated prisoner, and yet, he has more honor, more nobility, than any other man in this room."

"He is the Pendragon," Alcfrith said, with more starch in her voice than Rhiann had heard in many years. "Cadfael can't change that, even by killing him."

Rhiann's father snorted a laugh into his cup before draining it. He didn't even slap the women down, so sure was he of his own omnipotence. "You may keep your dreams." He pushed himself to his feet and turned to leave. "The dragon is chained; the prophecy dead."

Rhiann had heard about Cadwaladr her whole life. As a child, men in Cadfael's court had spoken of him as if he were a demon from the Underworld, or worse, a Saxon, coming to steal their home like a thief in the night. Later on, as she began to piece the story together, she realized that he was only a little older than she was, twenty-two now to her twenty, and their words said more about their own fears than Cadwaladr's power.

Rhiann's father had married Cadwaladr's mother after Cadwallon's death in battle, many miles from Aberffraw. The High Council of Wales had wanted peace in Gwynedd, in order to focus the concerted attention of all the native British rulers on the threat of the encroaching Saxons. Throughout Rhiann's life, the Saxon kingdoms had been growing in number and power. Two centuries before, the British kings had invited them in, but once here, could not control them. The Saxons had overrun nearly all of what had been British lands only a few generations before.

By now, everyone knew that the Saxons wouldn't ever return to their ancestral lands across the water. Her father, Cadfael, and Cadwallon before him, had allied with Penda of Mercia, but it had left a sour taste in the collective mouth of their people. All the Cymry knew that it was only a matter of time before the Saxons turned their gaze covetously on Wales.

The Council had settled upon Cadfael as the man to impose peace amid the chaos of constant war, provided Alcfrith agreed to the marriage. Rhiann suspected that *agreed* was too generous a word, and like most noble women, Alcfrith had had little choice in the matter. While the High Kingship had never materialized, and he didn't even rule all Gwynedd like Cadwallon before him, Cadfael did control a significant piece of it: Cadwaladr's birthright, as he'd said.

What Alcfrith had not done upon her marriage was give up her son, instead sending him away to be raised by another. Rhiann's father had raged at Alcfrith time and again, demanding to know to whom she'd given him. Alcfrith had refused to say, and perhaps that was the bargain she'd made—safety for her son, in exchange for her allegiance.

And now Cadwaladr was here, walking into the lion's den, although not quite of his own accord. Cadfael had spies everywhere and had known of his coming. The story he'd put out was that Cadwaladr's small band had forded the Menai Strait and met Cadfael's army just shy of Bryn Celliddu. Cadfael hadn't even bothered to meet the force himself, instead delegating the task to lesser men.

But Rhiann wasn't so sure, especially now that she'd heard Cadwaladr's exchange with her father. Before the feast, she'd questioned some of the older men in the garrison, particularly those who'd held allegiance to Cadwaladr's father once upon a time. A few of them had muttered among themselves about the evil Cadfael's acts would bring to Gwynedd. One even mentioned that he'd seen demons in the woods surrounding Aberffraw. The others had dismissed that as fantasy, and then together they'd rebuffed Rhiann's questions, as they had every right to do. Yet each, individually, had given her a look—like he wanted to speak—but thought better of it. Why had Cadwaladr come, only to be defeated so easily? Why had he sacrificed his men for such a fleeting chance?

And sacrifice them he had. Cadwaladr was the only survivor.

* * * * *

Rhiann pushed open the door to the room. Cadfael was keeping Cadwaladr in a third floor chamber, stripped of every piece of furniture. Cadwaladr huddled in a corner by the dark fireplace, the bread beside him uneaten. The window above his head had been left open—whether by him or her father Rhiann didn't know—but Cadwaladr hadn't tried to escape that way. Given that the drop to the ground was considerable, Rhiann wondered if her father hadn't left the window open to tempt Cadwaladr to leap from it, as a way out of the death that faced him tomorrow.

Cadwaladr looked up as Rhiann entered and straightened his back against the wall. His gaze was steady. As before in the great hall, it was difficult to look away from him. Rhiann shut the door on the guard who followed a few paces behind her.

"Knock when you're done with him." He dropped the bar on the heavy oak door.

Rhiann imagined him smirking behind the door, but she didn't care. Her position in the household was so low that to fall a little farther could hardly matter. She turned to the young man on the floor. "Lord Cadwaladr."

"Call me Cade. I've not earned my title." He paused. "Yet." He moistened his lips. Scabs had formed on them from the beating he'd received.

"Don't." Rhiann hastened forward with her cloth and washing bowl. "You'll start them bleeding again."

Cade licked his lower lip again anyway, prompting Rhiann to make an irritated face at him, annoyed that he was yet another male who routinely ignored whatever she said in order to do the exact opposite.

"Who are you?" Cade said.

"Rhiannon. Though everyone calls me Rhiann. I'm here to see to your wounds."

"Why?"

"You are Cadwaladr ap Cadwallon," Rhiann said. "Your very name testifies to the truth of your claim to be the last Pendragon."

"Cadwaladr." He laughed under his breath and shook his head. "*Battle-leader* my father may have christened me, but today the name bore false witness."

"I don't know about that." Rhiann crouched in front of Cade and put her cloth to a jagged cut on his forehead. It was a task she'd done for innumerable others: men such as he wounded in battle, or in a fight, or in any of a hundred other mistakes that left men battered and bloody. She was pleased to see that Cade's wounds were already healing well. Cade flinched when she touched him, however, and made to push her hand away.

"There's no need," he said.

"My father sent me to you. He has sought your death all my life. The better you look, the more glory your end confers on him."

Cade had been watching her face as she ministered to him and now leaned forward to grab the fist that held the cloth and stop her movements. "You're my sister?"

They wasted three heartbeats in a silent tug-of-war with the bloody cloth, but Rhiann persisted, and Cade finally gave up, releasing her.

Rhiann shook her head, dabbing at his forehead again. "No. My mother is not yours. She was my father's mistress and died at my birth, not long after he married your mother. You are two years older than I am."

Cade sat back. At his apparent acceptance, Rhiann took a moment to study him as he was studying her. She knew what he saw: dark eyes and black hair, pale skin and straight teeth. She looked nothing like her father or her dead mother, her nurse had told her. As a child, she'd hoped that she was a changeling and dreamed of the day her true family would come to take her away.

Rhiann also looked nothing like any of the daughters Cade's mother had produced with Cadfael. They were blond like she was, harking back to the northern blood of her ancestors. Yet Cade little resembled Alcfrith either, and Rhiann wondered at his long dead father. Was he as tall? Were his shoulders as broad and his hair as dark as Cade's? Did he draw the attention of everyone in a room to him as Cade did? It was only his eyes he must have gotten from his mother, although hers were a pale blue, like a washed out winter sky, and his were brighter and more piercing.

"I noticed you standing behind your father's chair." Cade released Rhiann from the spell that meeting his eyes had put her under. She moved back, setting down the bowl to rinse the cloth in the warm water. "If not for the fine weave of your dress, I'd have thought you were one of his slaves."

"I'm hardly more than that, in truth," Rhiann said. "My father demands that I serve him."

"And you do not wish to?"

"He murders you tomorrow, Cade," she said, by way of explanation. "And you are hardly the first."

"So you're a prisoner of a kind as well." Cade reached out as if to touch the back of Rhiann's hand with his finger. He held his hand above hers, touching but not touching, and then withdrew. "How am I to die?"

"Hanging," Rhiann said. "They're building the gallows now. Are you much wounded elsewhere?"

Cade shrugged and rested the back of his head against the wall. "Only a few bruises. And my pride."

Able suddenly to give voice to her anger, Rhiann threw down her cloth. "Why? Why did you come here?"

Cade canted his head to one side to look at her. "Why do you care?"

Rhiann gazed at him, exasperated. "Because we've been waiting! The people of Gwynedd have been waiting for twenty years for you to come, and we would have gladly waited for many more until you were ready, rather than have you die tomorrow by my father's will."

Cade shook his head. "You don't know, do you?" His voice was barely above a whisper, and Rhiann leaned in closer to hear him better.

"Know what?" she said.

Cade shook his head again. "Never mind. It doesn't matter now."

"It does matter," Rhiann said, feeling fierce. "What does the bard sing of Arthur? *Fear and dread followed him, even to his death?* That describes my father just as well. You shouldn't be dying here for nothing."

"*Fear and dread followed him, even to his death, before we covered him with earth. Yet death do I prefer to cowardice. For this bitter death, I lament,*" Cade quoted. "I know that Arthur cast a shadow far longer than mine ever could, but I would be such a one as fought at his side."

"Arthur is dead, Cade," Rhiann said. "And you'll die tomorrow. There's not much there for the bards to sing of."

Cade gave her a blank stare, which she met. The she looked away. "I'm sorry."

Cade sat silent, and then he sighed hard, forcing the air out of his chest. "I am less of a man for telling you, but my heart tells me that I must speak to someone, even if she is only a girl-who-is-not-my-sister."

He studied Rhiann again, and she waited, feeling like she was finally going to be told the truth, and perhaps it was only a stranger such as he who could tell it. "Rhiannon," he said, surprising her by using her formal name, "your father invited me here."

Rhiann's hand jerked, and she nearly spilled the bowl of water. "He what?"

Cade gave her a rueful look. "We were to meet at the ford of the Cefni River, here on Anglesey. We've been negotiating our meeting for weeks."

"I'm sure nobody but my father and a few advisors knew that. There's been no talk; no gossip."

Cade shrugged. "I was clearly a fool to believe him, and even more of one to come here, but it was not without cause. After I took from him one of his forts on the mainland of Gwynedd, he sent an emissary to me. He said that he didn't have an heir and would bestow the honor upon me, given that my mother is his wife. But he felt he needed to meet me first. You must admit, this overture was not without precedent and, after my initial skepticism, I believed him."

"He—" Rhiann swallowed hard through the thickening in her throat. She could barely get the words out. "Nobody who knows my father would ever have believed him. He hates you with such passion I've thought at times his heart would give out when he speaks of you."

"I didn't have the benefit of your experience," Cade said, "nor the advice of counselors who would know better. Even my foster father agreed that I should make the attempt. Unfortunately, he, along with the other counselors I did have, paid for their ignorance and my naïveté with their lives."

Not wanting to think about their wasteful deaths, Rhiann bowed her head, soaking and squeezing the cloth over and over again. Finally, Cade reached out a hand and gently took it from her. This time, she let him.

"I'm sorry," Rhiann said again.

"And my mother?" Cade said. "How goes it with her?"

Now it was Rhiann's turn to shake her head. "You've not seen her? Not since you were an infant?"

"No. Not until today."

Rhiann didn't know what to say; how to begin or not begin. "I don't know. She has never—" She paused and tried again. "I have lived with her my whole life, and she showed more emotion in seeing you than I have ever seen from her. For the first time it occurs to me that she didn't give you away, she gave away herself. She sent you away and kept herself from you so that you might live."

Cade stared past Rhiann at the fireless hearth, and she followed his gaze. It was the beginning of February, but even so, not too chilly in the room, despite the recent rains. Rhiann supposed the guards would not have lit the fire anyway for fear of finding the fort burning down around them in the night. Then Cade flexed his large hands, and Rhiann imagined him grasping a sword and wielding it. Even the heavier Saxon ones would give him little difficulty.

"Go now, and do not watch tomorrow. I would not have you see me—" He stopped and cleared his throat. "I'd prefer you didn't see what happens to me tomorrow."

Rhiann had been kneeling on the floor but now got to her feet, leaving the bowl and cloth in case he wanted them. "Shall I send for your mother?"

Cade didn't answer. Rhiann let the silence lengthen and then turned to the door because it didn't seem like he was going to respond. She knocked so the guard would let her out.

"No," he said, finally. He remained sprawled in his original position on the floor.

Rhiann nodded. The guard opened the door to allow her to leave and then barred it behind her. The guard had once been one of Cadwallon's men, long since retired from the field and now reduced to guarding his former lord's son. He refused to meet her eyes, but spoke anyway.

"It's best this way, miss," he said.

"No, it isn't." The fierceness of before rose inside her again. "This is wrong. I can't believe I'm the only one who sees it!"

The man shrank back under Rhiann's attack, but before he could say anything more, Rhiann felt a step on the floorboards behind her. She turned to see Alcfrith watching them from the other end of the hall. Their eyes met, and Alcfrith tipped her head towards the entrance to her room before entering it. She left the door ajar.

Hesitantly, Rhiann followed her into the room and shut the door.

"You've seen him?" Alcfrith said.

"Yes."

"Is he badly hurt?"

"He's not much injured. Far less than I feared. He will certainly live long enough for Father to murder him."

"As he murdered Cadwaladr's father," Alcfrith said.

"What? What did you say?" Rhiann said. "My father killed Cadwallon?"

Alcfrith turned to Rhiann with a blank stare, one that told Rhiann she was already so far gone in grief she didn't see her—and perhaps her words had not been meant for Rhiann, but for the woman Alcfrith had been.

"You must save Cadwaladr," she said, "and leave Aberffraw with him."

"Me?" Rhiann said. "I've been struggling with how it might be possible since they brought him in, but I'm afraid it isn't."

"You have no future here," Alcfrith said, ignoring Rhiann's protest. "You've turned down all the men your father has brought for you to marry."

"I couldn't marry any of them," Rhiann said. "They were all his allies. Every last one was old and evil. Did you see the teeth on Meurig of Rhiannt?"

Alcfrith shook her head. "Marriage could have been a way out of here for you. As it is, it's too late. If you stay here, your father will force you to marry Peada, my brother's son. He's not a bad man, but no Christian."

"I've already told father I won't marry Peada," Rhiann said. "The priest won't let Father force me into it."

"Peada is the ruler of Middle Anglia and King Penda's son. When Peada comes for you, you will have no choice. He does not listen to priests."

Rhiann's stomach sank into her boots. All along she'd feared exactly that, even if she hadn't admitted it to herself and had managed to defy her father up until now. Cadfael had known it too, undoubtedly. He'd taken the opportunity to punish Rhiann with public disgrace for her disobedience, but Rhiann had felt throughout it all that he'd been laughing at her, sure in his power over her future.

Every man he'd brought to Aberffraw to seek Rhiann's hand had been Welsh, and thus subject to the restrictions of the Church. The Saxons, on the other hand, were pagans, bowing only to their gods and with no respect for the gods of others. They'd sacked churches and killed monks countless times. Of course, Cadfael's men would have done the same to them, if they'd had churches.

The Welsh gods, the *sidhe*, were entirely different from the Saxon gods, with familiar names that didn't grate on one's ears: Arianrhod and Gwydion, children of Dôn; Llyr, god of the sea; Arawn, Lord of Annwn, the Underworld. Rhiann suspected that many of her father's men, under their Christian guise, still believed in the old gods, keeping them close but hidden like a comfortable and faded shirt worn beneath a new and glossy coat of mail. Since the coming of the Christ, the *sidhe* had hidden themselves, no longer walking freely among their people. With each passing year, they retreated further into the mists and shadows of the high valleys and mountains.

"I hadn't realized that my time was so short," Rhiann said. "Father hasn't said anything to me about it." Her father claimed to be a Christian, but an alliance with a Saxon king was worth more to him than his religion. Or her.

"Why would he?" Alcfrith said. "You are a woman, and your value is found in what he can sell you for, even at twenty and long past the point at which you should have married. You are his to do with as he pleases." She turned her back on Rhiann, her head bowed. "Just as I am."

Uncertain, Rhiann reached out a tentative hand and rested it on Alcfrith's shoulder. Alcfrith took Rhiann's hand in hers, turned back, and managed a half-smile.

"I may not be able to save myself," she said, "but I will not stand by to see either Cadwaladr or you lose your life, or your soul, at Cadfael's hands."

"I don't know what to say." Rhiann was stunned at Alcfrith's frankness. "You've spoken more to me in these few moments than in my entire life."

"I have clothes for you." Alcfrith turned abruptly from Rhiann. She walked to a chest in the corner of the chamber and opened it. Inside were male garments—breeches, jersey and cloak—which Alcfrith brought out one by one and piled into Rhiann's arms.

"Why are you doing this?" Rhiann said.

"I've never been a mother to you." Alcfrith closed the lid to the chest and faced Rhiann again. "Neither to you nor to my son."

"I never expected—"

"Well you should have!" Alcfrith said.

Startled, Rhiann took a step back.

"All your life until now you've held yourself cheaply, expecting nothing and receiving nothing," Alcfrith said. "I treated you no differently than your father did. I just couldn't bear—" She paused.

"Bear what?"

Alcfrith took a deep breath and let it out. "You reminded me so much of Cadwaladr, even as an infant: so stubborn, so fiery, and yet so soft and warm in my arms. I couldn't bear to hold you. As you grew—as you crawled and walked and talked—all I could see in you was my lost son."

"You can see him now," Rhiann said. "He's right next door."

"No." Alcfrith shook her head. "I have no claim on him. He owes me nothing, and I will not ask anything from him because he'd give it."

Alcfrith was right. Rhiann had spoken with Cade for the first time that evening and yet she already knew him well enough to know that what Alcfrith said was true. "Father's not going to kill Cadwaladr," Rhiann said, suddenly sure.

Alcfrith nodded. "I have a plan. God willing, you will take him out of here and never see me again. If Cadfael catches you, I will not be able to save either one of you."

"I understand," Rhiann said.

"You don't have much time, *cariad*."

Rhiann stared at her. *Loved one*, Alcfrith had called her, for the first time in her life. Alcfrith put a hand on each of Rhiann's shoulders, pulled her into her arms for a brief hug, and then stepped back in order to look deep into Rhiann's eyes.

"There is much you need to do," Alcfrith said.

Sweet Mary, do I dare?

Yet Rhiann did exactly as Alcfrith asked.

2

Cade

Rhiann's footsteps faded down the passage. Cade remained where she'd left him, staring up at the rafters above his head. He wondered if his father had ever contemplated the same wooden beams, although Cadwallon had made the fortress at Dinas Bran his primary seat when he was High King, not Aberffraw, here on the Isle of Anglesey. If his father had been here, Cade couldn't sense it. Pain, loneliness, and despair were all he felt from the walls. It wasn't too much of a stretch to think they were merely reflecting his own feelings back at him.

Rhiannon. Cade had told her that he'd noticed her behind her father's chair, but *notice* wasn't quite the word he should have used. He'd sensed her gaze on him before he reached the dais. He'd remained aware of her, there on the periphery of his vision, impossible to dismiss or ignore, throughout his subsequent conversation with Cadfael. She might not realize it, but everyone else in the room knew that the idea of her as a serving wench was laughable. Cadfael, the fool, had no notion of what he had on his hands. Or perhaps he did and sought to quell her—or even break her—if he could. Cade shook his head at the thought. Perhaps the odds were long, but he was betting on Rhiann.

He raised his hands above his head to study them. The bruising was all but gone, and he had a flash of unaccustomed gratitude—in contrast to his usual loathing—towards the power that curled within him, tamed now, but still sending out tendrils of energy that Cade fought constantly to contain. Cade touched a hand to his lip. He'd enjoyed Rhiann's ministrations, but in truth, he was healing just fine without her. If he were here at dawn, which he had no intention of being, Cadfael would be pleased.

Cade had already quartered the room before Rhiann arrived and come up with exactly one avenue of escape: the window. Now, he got to his feet to check it again. Looking down, he acknowledged that he could jump the distance, but to what end? The activity continued in the courtyard on the other side of the building. If he did reach the ground, the men-at-arms who watched the gate would be after him before he'd run ten paces. He might be able to fight them off, kill them all as he could have killed the two guards in Cadfael's hall, but if the gate was closed, he would be no closer to freedom than he was now. Even he couldn't batter through solid wood.

Cade leaned far out the window, still unable to see anything from this vantage point—not even the gallows of which Rhiann had spoken—other than the high wooden fence that faced him. He eyed the distance to the fence. Jumping the thirty feet separating him from the balustrade might not be beyond his abilities, but the impact when he hit it might send him right through the wooden planks.

I'll bide my time until midnight has passed. The guards will be tired and everyone else in bed. Resolved to wait, Cade returned to the floor and closed his eyes, letting his thoughts drift into the darker corners and reaches of his mind.

* * * * *

"Tap ... tap ... tap ..."

Cade opened his eyes to the burned-out fire and darkened room. He pushed to his feet, straightening his spine, which was stiff from holding the same position for so long. As before, a faint light came from beneath the door.

"Tap ... tap ... tap ..."

Crouching, Cade peered through a crack between two slats in the wood. "Who's there?"

"Madoc."

Cade thought back through his acquaintances for someone named Madoc who could be alive and here and came up blank.

"I was one of your father's men-at-arms."

"Will you unlatch the door?" Cade said, getting to the only point that was of any interest to him.

"That's not the plan," Madoc said. "The other guard has gone to relieve himself, so we haven't much time."

"Time for what?" Cade said.

"Your mother asks you to look out your window."

My mother? My window?

Cade strode from the door to the window. He'd closed but not latched the wooden shutters earlier, and now pulled them open, revealing a clear night and a full moon. He'd been lost in his thoughts far longer than he'd intended and perhaps only three hours remained before dawn.

He looked down. Aberffraw stood on a high mound, surrounded by a wooden palisade and deep trench. To the northeast flowed a river Cade couldn't see from his window. Beyond that lay a forest, and to the west and south, the sea. Between the house and the fence Cade could make out nothing but shadows in the dark. Then one of the shapes moved and coalesced into a human form.

"Cade!"

"Rhiann!"

She pushed back the hood of her cloak, so he could see her better. She wore men's clothes: boots, breeches, and shirt. At the sight of her, hope rose in Cade, but he instantly suppressed it.

"Catch!" Rhiann's arm swung like a pendulum, and Cade leaned out the window to grab the rope she threw to him.

Trying to hurry while at the same time keeping quiet, he turned to look over the room. It contained no furniture to which he might tie the rope, but the supporting beams of the building were stronger than furniture would have been anyway. One of the rafters that supported the roof stretched from above the door in the opposite wall to a point just above the window. Cade reached up to it and hung on it, testing its ability to hold his weight. It held him easily, without shifting or sagging, so he looped the rope over it and tied it tight.

Cade glanced once at Rhiann who stood with her white face upturned. Committed now to the endeavor, he lifted one leg over the rim of the window, tugged once on the rope to test its strength and that of his knot, and then began to climb down. Rhiann had thoughtfully knotted the rope every two feet, sparing his hands a burn. Cade walked his feet down the wall, moving hand under hand, and then dropped the last six feet. He landed hard, glad his captors hadn't taken his boots when they'd confiscated his weapons.

"I hope that didn't wake the household," Cade said in a hoarse whisper.

"We want them awake," Rhiann said.

"We do?" Cade opened his mouth to ask for an explanation, but Rhiann shushed him with a hand on his arm and a finger to his lips, touching him again like no one had touched him in years. For good reason.

"Not now. You'll see." Rhiann handed Cade a cloak, which he threw over his shoulders, and then surprised him with a belt and sword.

"What's this?" Cade strapped the belt around his waist.

"You'll need that sword wherever you're going," she said. "I'm sorry I couldn't find the one that my father took from you, but this one was in the armory in a chest, unused. As freeing you will surely anger my father, the donation of a sword seemed a small matter."

"Why are you doing this?"

Rhiann shook her head, choosing not to answer. Instead, she grabbed Cade's hand—oblivious to the threat to her or the cost to him—and led him along the side of the building, coming to a halt at the corner of the keep. Cade peered over her shoulder and found the reason for the inattention of the guards, Rhiann's unconcern about the noise they had made, and her notion that he would more easily escape with everyone in the fort awake.

The stables were on fire.

"It was your mother's idea," Rhiann said, almost apologetically. "It was all we could think of to draw attention away from your escape."

"By all that is holy, you are reckless," Cade said.

They stood in the shadows, waiting for more men to fill the courtyard and provide them with cover and confusion. It didn't take long. Within a count of fifty, the space between them and the stables was a seething mass of men and horses. As the whinnying horses were freed from the stables one by one, Cade recognized his own horse, Cadfan, racing past.

He stepped out of the shadows, and Rhiann released his hand.

"Go!" she said.

Cade didn't need any further urging. He ran forward to intercept Cadfan. The horse had no bridle, so Cade grabbed his mane and threw himself onto his back. Head low, sprawled across the stallion's neck, Cade held on as

Cadfan galloped toward the gate, which had been opened to allow a chain of people with water buckets to snake out of the fort and down the pathway to a stream. Cade followed them, staying low on the horse and as far out of the torchlight as he could.

As soon as he passed through the gate, Cade turned Cadfan away from the workers, following the palisade to the east. Cadfan had calmed by the time the darkness enveloped them fully and Cade headed him for the stream. As they splashed through the water and crossed to the other side, Cade sat up to look back. A glow from the burning stables lit the sky, but from where he sat, it appeared the fire had not spread.

Without a doubt, Rhiann's father would curse the expense of rebuilding the stables. What he would do when he discovered the loss of his prisoner, Cade didn't know, but he could guess. Cadfael would never be able to say, however, that he hadn't invited Cade in.

Cade felt a moment's pang for Rhiann's safety. It was a welcome change from fearing for his own. Now that he had escaped, the exhilaration was ebbing, leaving him with the sick, shocked feelings he'd had before: at Cadfael's betrayal; at the death of his friends and companions; at his imprisonment. The actions of Rhiann and his mother simply added to his bewilderment.

Cade looked for Rhiann among the human chain that carried water to the fire, not wanting to disappear without thanking her, but knowing that she wouldn't want her night's work wasted and him caught. Even as he hesitated, she ran down the path towards him, leading another horse and carrying an extra bridle for Cadfan in her hand.

"What are you doing?" Cade took the reins she offered and hastily looped them over Cadfan's head.

"Coming with you."

"Rhiannon," Cade said, his voice low and urgent. "You can't possibly."

"I have to. Your mother insisted on it. There's no future for me at Aberffraw."

"It's your home."

"It has never been a home for me, only a prison." Rhiann mounted her horse and turned his head away from the fort. "Besides, you don't know this country. If I let you go alone, you'll stumble about in the dark until you're captured again, and all this work will be for nothing."

Cade's night vision was exceptional, but she couldn't know that, and he found it hard to argue with her. Worse, he found that he didn't want to argue with her. "We must cross the Strait and reach the mainland. Those lands I know, and from there I can lead us to safety."

"Where is safety from the King of Gwynedd?" she said.

"Dinas Emrys," he said.

"That's my father's fort, isn't it?"

"Not anymore," Cade said.

Realizing they were running out of time and that he didn't have the words to force her back to Aberffraw, Cade spurred Cadfan forward into the trees that formed a dark barrier on the other side of the stream. Rhiann followed and pointed them along a path that wound through the trees.

"This leads to Gwalchmai, a small settlement some five miles inland from Aberffraw," she said. "We should probably find a different road before that, as I don't know how quickly my father will send riders to pursue us."

"We might have a little time before they discover my absence," Cade said. "No doubt they will organize a search, for you as well as for me."

They rode far more slowly than Cade would have liked, but it was dark under the trees. It took some effort to focus on the lane ahead and avoid any obstacles in their path. After two miles, the pair turned off the first road onto a smaller one that would bring them to the Menai Strait. Soon, they would reach the point where Rhiann's father had ambushed Cade and his men. Cade glanced at Rhiann, but she was concentrating hard, and he left her to her thoughts, focusing instead on dark memories of his own.

We cross the Strait at low tide, ferried in boats rented for that purpose. The oarsmen refuse to look at me, but my thoughts are elsewhere, and I choose not to read more into their actions than I think they warrant. A mistake.

Once on the Anglesey side of the Strait, we ride along the road to Aberffraw in good formation. The clouds above our heads are thick with rain, although the deluge has stopped for now. I am wary, but in good spirits.

Cadfael's priest is among us, surety for the pact Cadfael swears he'll make with me. The priest has made himself useful throughout our journey, blessing our departure, blessing the waters as we crossed them, and swearing on the piece of the True Cross I wear around my neck that he will ensure my well-being until we reach Cadfael. His sycophantic nature rubs me the wrong way, but I ignore it, believing him sincere.

Perhaps he was.

The February sun comes out from behind a cloud and is unaccountably bright. It flashes down on the priest, who is bowing and smiling at me for perhaps the one-hundredth time, before disappearing again. Although my hood shades my eyes, I wince at the momentary brightness. Distracted by the priest, my foster-father, Cynyr, leans forward to speak.

And with that, the forest erupts around us.

The first arrows pierce our ranks. Cadfan screams and rears. I instantly lose track of both the priest and Cynyr.

"Retreat!" I shout, realizing too late that we have walked into a trap and are vastly outnumbered. I turn Cadfan's head in order to flee back the way we came, but as I urge Cadfan forward, Cadfael's men block the road behind us. They don't even bother to hide their colors, mocking me with his banner, which he openly displays, wanting me to understand who comes against me.

Deion, one of my captains, takes his place beside me. He has cut through four of our attackers. The bloodlust of battle has blinded me to everything but the sword in my hand and the men who have died upon it, but I come to myself at his approach, aware of my downed men and that we are losing. Then, a fresh company of Cadfael's men surges from the woods to surround us.

"Halt!" Cadfael's captain shouts.

I had raised my sword, ready to continue the fight, but arrest the motion. Both of my last two men are on the *ground now, a sword to their throats. I lower my sword in the faint hope that I can save them by my surrender.*

The captain saunters toward me, arrogance in every line of his body. "Do you admit defeat?" he asks, gesturing to my companions. "I will spare them if you submit."

I nod. Within moments, I am on the ground myself. A soldier ties my hands behind my back and bloodies my face with an errant boot. As even the great Arthur himself once found, strength can be defeated by treachery. The captain smiles as he hauls me to my feet and pulls me towards a wagon that will carry me to Aberffraw.

He glances over his shoulder. "Kill the others."

Only death, whether his or mine, will spare Cadfael my revenge.

Cade glanced at Rhiann. The woods were thicker along the smaller road, but they had moved more quickly than his best hopes, once he accepted that he had Rhiann with him. "You've done well. This ride has not been easy."

"We still have a long way to go," she said. "Don't congratulate me just yet."

They reached the water's edge as dawn broke, not that it was much of a dawn. In the hours since Cade had stood in the window at Aberffraw, the clouds had come in to obscure the moon and now hung low to the ground. Soon it would begin to drizzle. Cade stared across the Strait, peering through the gray mist to the mainland of Gwynedd and feeling unrelieved tension in the pit of his stomach.

He studied the water. It flowed southeast, indicating that the tide was going out. The best time to cross the Strait was when the water was at its calmest, approximately one hour before high or low tide. That ideal time would be soon. Grown men and ships had foundered in the unexpectedly strong currents, even when the water was less than ten feet deep and only two hundred yards across at its narrowest point. Here, it was much deeper and wider. Cade eyed the distance, calculating the effort it would take to cross it.

"You mean to swim it here?" Rhiann said.

"There is nothing for it. We've no choice but to keep going." Cade looked her up and down. "We'll need to dismount and remove our clothing. It will only drag us down and ensure we die from exposure before noon."

Rhiann nodded.

Wordlessly, Cade stripped to his loincloth and she to hardly more—just braies, although she'd bound her breasts with a long strip of linen wrapped around her chest and tied in a knot at her breastbone. Cade stuffed the clothes into the saddlebags on Rhiann's horse and strapped his sword to the outside, next to a bow and quiver Rhiann had brought.

There, it wouldn't hinder the horse and would leave their hands free for swimming.

"You're trusting me too much for a man you've only just met, Rhiann." Cade deliberately didn't look at her as he cinched the strap around the bags more tightly.

"Are you a danger to me?"

Cade finally managed to look at her. Her eyes were watchful. The true answer was *yes*, but not for the reasons she thought. "No. I would protect you with my life."

"Then I am right to trust you, aren't I?" she said.

Cade just shook his head, finding her logic impeccable but her closeness nearly unbearable. *I could pull her to me, but then where would that leave us?* "Follow me. Can you swim?"

"Of course," she said, starch in her voice.

"I was just asking," Cade said. "Most women don't know how, you know."

"I'm not most women."

Cade choked on a laugh, unable to disagree, and then grasped Cadfan's mane. He pulled the horse down the muddy bank and urged him into the water, making sure Cadfan stayed to his right so the horse wouldn't knock him over in the current. Rhiann entered the water a few paces behind him.

The horses didn't like it, but they didn't balk. Talking softly, Cade and Rhiann walked them forward. After a dozen yards, the water was up to Cade's thighs and the current began to tug him into Cadfan. He stayed upright, with his left hand out for balance and his right caught in Cadfan's mane. It had been a long time since he'd been in water quite as cold as this.

Soon, the current lifted Cade's feet as the water rose to his chin, and he was forced to swim. Another few yards and Cadfan too was swimming. He outpaced Cade and rather than hinder him, Cade let go of his mane in order to concentrate on his own survival.

They were not quite halfway across when Rhiann gasped: "Cade!"

He looked behind them. Four men on horses rode forward and back on the Anglesey bank. Cade faced the mainland again. "Keep going. We mustn't stop."

One of the men called to Rhiann, his voice echoing above the rushing water: "My lady! Your father asks that you return to Aberffraw!"

Cade glanced at Rhiann, but she ignored the men, focusing instead on keeping her head above water. Another shout came from the bank, and Cade chanced a look back. The men had entered the water. More desperate now, he and

Rhiann pushed harder, taking long strokes. Rhiann was trying to keep up, and Cade slowed slightly, urging her to stay strong. They were nearly three-quarters of the way across by now, and Cade thought they should have been able to stand, but as he could not get his footing, Rhiann certainly couldn't either.

They swam another twenty yards. Rhiann's breathing became more labored with every stroke. Finally, Cadfan was able to run through the water, and Cade put his feet down again. He touched the sand and stood, finding the water was down to his hips. Rhiann gasped for breath beside him, coughing and numb from the cold. She staggered to her knees in the shallow water. With the water only to his hocks, Cadfan stopped and looked back at Cade. He almost seemed amused, and it was as if he was asking, *why exactly did we do this?*

Cade wrapped his arms around Rhiann's waist and pulled her to her feet, both of them so numb from the cold water that he almost couldn't feel her skin. Almost. Together they plunged forward, out of the water. Cade released Rhiann as they reached her horse and then ran to Cadfan. He grasped the reins and threw himself onto his back. Seated, he swung around to look at the men behind them. Their pursuers were in the middle of the Strait, with one of them obviously laboring badly.

"The one who can't swim is Eben, one of my father's knights." Rhiann, too, had mounted and turned back to the water. "I recognized him when he was on the far bank."

None of Cadfael's men appeared to be good swimmers. They swam heavy in the water too, so perhaps they hadn't had the foresight to strip off their clothes before entering the Strait. Water-filled boots were as good as an anchor around one's neck in that current. Cade brushed his sopping hair from his eyes and led Rhiann away, riding out of the water to the shore. The trees that grew down to the water's edge would provide them with a haven. They needed to lose their pursuers in these woods.

3

Rhiann

The rain fell in earnest now. Rhiann, wet all through, was so cold she couldn't feel her fingers. Fortunately, Cade allowed a stop once they'd put some distance between themselves and her father's men. They dismounted and hurriedly stripped off their wet undergarments and pulled on their dry clothes. Rhiann's wool cloak felt wonderful after the icy waters of the Strait.

"I'm sorry." Cade brushed his wet hair out of his face again. "This isn't going to get better any time soon."

"I know." Rhiann remounted her horse. "At least we're alive. My father intended to hang you at dawn."

Cade brightened at that. "So it's a good day already." With that, he turned and began walking with long strides, leading his horse through the brush and trees.

Rhiann was exhausted. The last time she'd felt this weary was after the birth of Alcfrith's stillborn daughter the previous summer. The midwife and she had stayed beside

Alcfrith's bed for two days. In that case, Rhiann had been emotionally drained as well as physically spent, and despair had been the order of the day.

With Cade, she felt exhilarated. She'd never done anything like this before and was astonished at her own audacity. *Can I be the same girl as yesterday? Has one of the sidhe come and tapped me on the shoulder to turn me into someone who would dare to burn down my father's stables to save his enemy?* Rhiann had never even been off the Isle of Anglesey before. Now a whole new world opened before her, with Cade at its center. By saving Cade, she had saved herself, just as Alcfrith had said.

Rhiann stared at Cade's back as he led his horse ahead of her along a trail that only he could see. He moved confidently through the forest, and she wondered if that was something she could learn, or at least learn to imitate. He no longer even seemed to feel his wounds. His stride was sure, and when he glanced back at her, perhaps aware of her scrutiny, she saw that the cuts and bruises on his face were gone. That shouldn't have been possible, even with the time in the salty water of the Strait.

"Should I dismount?" Rhiann said.

"Please don't." Cade held up his hand. "You're tired beyond words. It will be easier for me if you stay where you are."

"I can make my own way," she said. "I don't intend to be a burden to you."

Cade shot her a withering look. "How far would you get, then, without me? And what kind of man would I be to let you go, after all you've done?"

"I–" Rhiann began, unwilling to concede her helplessness, especially given all she'd managed so far, as Cade had said.

Cade cut her off. "Don't mention it again. I would not desert you, and I expect the same from you in return."

Oh. Well that was a different story entirely. "I wouldn't! I can be as loyal as any man."

"As loyal as those men back there?" Cade's mouth twisted into a wry smile.

Rhiann glanced behind her. Thick trees and bushes screened them from the men who stalked them. Cade and she had been traveling for a while, so her father's men should have come out of the water by now, but there was still no sign of pursuit. "Not like them."

Cade nodded. "I hold my men to a higher standard. It's not unthinking loyalty I want, so much as men who are capable of understanding my orders while they obey them. I don't want men to follow me blindly. I want them to obey me because I've earned their trust, and they have faith in me."

"My father expects blindness," Rhiann said. "He wants me simply to obey him, as if I had no thoughts of my own in my head."

"Well now you get to listen to me instead," Cade said, matter-of-factly. "Do you know the country here?"

"No," she said. "Do you?"

Cade's expression turned thoughtful. "I've spent these last weeks since I took Dinas Emrys scouting the land between the fort and the Strait. I know where we are, and where we need to go."

"So you weren't entirely sure of my father after all," Rhiann said.

"I wasn't completely stupid," Cade said.

"I didn't say you were! I just—" Rhiann paused, wondering what she did think.

"I walked into a trap I should have seen," Cade said. "I lost all of my men. I lost the only father I've ever known. There is no pain greater than that, and you cannot chastise me more than I have berated myself."

"I didn't mean that," Rhiann said. "I've lived so long in fear of my father that I find it hard to believe that others exist who wouldn't fear him, who wouldn't know to fear him."

"Well, I know him now and am alive to learn from our encounter." Cade swatted a branch out of his way. "Thanks to you."

"Who was your foster father?" Rhiann blurted out the question, one everyone at Aberffraw had posed a thousand times before without an answer. "Where did your mother hide you?"

Cade glanced back at her, a small smile playing around his lips. "I can't believe you still don't know because the secret wasn't well kept these last few years. I'm almost tempted not to tell you, but you'd discover it soon enough."

"Where?" she asked again.

"Far enough so that I wasn't under Cadfael's nose," Cade said, "but not so far I wouldn't have my boots planted firmly in the soil of Gwynedd. My mother is a Saxon, but she refused to deny me my birthright. Taliesin brought me to my father's vassal, Cynyr, lord of Bryn y Castell."

"No wonder we never knew where you'd been taken," Rhiann said. "Lord Cynyr never pledged his allegiance to my father. That stuck in Cadfael's craw, I can assure you."

"Cynyr's wife lost a child to sickness only days before Cadfael married my mother, or so I've been told," Cade said. "They put out that he'd recovered and then raised me as their own, under their dead son's name."

"When did you learn that you were Cadwallon's son and the true heir to Gwynedd?" Rhiann said.

"Cynyr spoke to me of my destiny when I was twelve and ready to hear it," Cade said. "It was both a surprise, and not. Others within the household had known, you see, and people gossip."

"I learned by mistake that I was illegitimate," Rhiann said. "For the longest time, I'd thought Alcfrith was my mother, until I heard the cook lamenting about how skinny I was, *even for a royal bastard.*"

"I'd decided I was a bastard," Cade said, "because I'd overheard someone speaking of my foster brother, Rhun, as the true son of the household."

"Did Rhun mind, once he knew who you really were?"

"He could have resented me terribly," Cade said, "but he didn't. He is only a year older than I, and has been my closest companion all my life."

"Did he ... was he also killed in the battle?" Rhiann said hesitantly, hating to think that Cade had lost his brother as well as his father.

"No," Cade said, shortly. "He awaits us at Dinas Emrys. Rhun is not a Christian."

Rhiann sucked in a breath. "If my father had known, he would never have let him enter his house. He might have killed him on the spot."

Cade snorted a laugh. "Instead he killed his own priest, who had traveled with us as proof of your father's good faith."

Rhiann felt her eyes go wide. "I didn't know that."

Cade checked Rhiann's face and then turned back to the trail. "There is an ancient chapel near Bryn y Castell. It stands over a natural spring long revered as a holy site. I went there to pray for assistance before I journeyed to Anglesey. Rhun laughed at me for it. It crossed my mind as the first of your father's arrows hit us, that Rhun was right to mock. Now, however ... now I'm not so sure."

Rhiann started to reply, even to assure him of her own belief, when Cade held up a hand to silence her. They listened together, and then he motioned for her to dismount. Believing absolutely that he knew more of the woods than she, Rhiann closed her mouth and dropped as silently as she could to the ground. The layers of leaves that had muffled the sounds of their steps would do the same for any pursuers.

Rhiann listened hard with Cade, feeling, more than hearing, the quiet under the trees. Although she was not a woodsman, she knew to be careful when the small sounds were silenced.

Cade pointed to the bow Rhiann had strapped to her horse. "Can you shoot that?" He kept his voice low.

"It's too big for me," she said. "I wish I could have brought mine, but I took this from the armory for you. Some men feel as naked without a bow as a blade."

"I do always prefer to have both," Cade said.

He stroked his horse's nose reassuringly and then stepped to Rhiann's side in order to untie the bow from the saddlebags. Rhiann helped him strap the quiver onto his back and then rifled through the saddlebags to find the bowstrings. On top of them were the apples Rhiann had brought, and she looked longingly at them.

Cade shook his head. "Can you wait? Apples make too much noise when you bite into them."

It was such a mundane observation that she almost laughed, but sobered instantly, saddened to see that the loaf of bread she'd included had disintegrated in the water. Putting her hunger aside, she retrieved the sack containing the bowstrings, thankful that they had remained dry within their leather casing.

"You can shoot a bow, then?" Cade fitted the string to the bow and tied the ends.

"My father doesn't have a son and has lamented that fact every day of his reign," Rhiann said. "Several years ago, he taught me to shoot, as an ill-humored jest I think, because he had no son to teach. I continued on my own because ... I wanted to, and a woman might have a need to defend herself."

"I grant you that. Like right now." Without asking, he put his hand to her waist and pulled out the belt knife she always kept there. He bent his head to meet her eyes. "Can you use this if you have to?"

"Yes. That too my father was willing to make sure of." It wasn't for her, of course, that Cadfael had done so, but because an assault on his daughter would besmirch his honor as much as her own.

"Don't hesitate," Cade said, echoing the words of Rhiann's long-ago instructor.

"I know," she said.

Cade put out a hand, palm down. "Stay low; stay quiet."

Rhiann nodded. She tried to track him with her eyes as he made his way through the woods but in a blink of an eye, he'd slipped away.

In his absence, the air under the trees became oppressive. The rain continued to *drip, drip, drip* from the leafless branches above. Many times in late winter and early spring, the drizzle was so unrelenting at Aberffraw she thought she'd go mad if she spent another day without the sun. Now, she listened hard to distinguish between the natural sound of the rain in the trees and something that might be unnatural, like the plopping of raindrops on metal or leather.

Her horse blew air from his nostrils, and Rhiann stroked his cheek to calm him. He could sense her unease, and she strove to damp it down. She leaned forward so her head rested on his and tried to take deep breaths. They stood together, listening, for a hundred heartbeats, Rhiann counting them out one by one. Then the horse raised his head, and at that moment Rhiann felt motion behind her.

She made to spin around, knife extended, but reacted too late.

"Hello, missy." An iron-strong arm slipped around her waist as the voice spoke in her ear. Rhiann slashed down and back with the knife, but the man caught her wrist with his free hand before she could connect. "Now, now. We can't have that."

He squeezed her wrist until she gasped in pain and released the knife. It dropped to the ground, instantly becoming lost among the leaves at the base of the tree. The horses stamped nervously, and the man pulled her backwards, away from them, wrenching her arms behind her back at the same time.

Rhiann stumbled, but managed to catch her breath anyway. "Cade! Ca—"

The man cut off her words with a hand to her mouth. She growled at him, and tried to bite him as she struggled to pull away. She managed to get one of his fingers between her teeth.

"*Mochyn budr*!" He threw Rhiann from him.

She fell to the ground, hands out to brace against the impact. The moment she hit the earth, she pushed off, but again the man was quicker, and his full weight came down on her back. He had one of her wrists in each of his hands and forced her to stretch them out to each side, so that she lay in the shape of a cross beneath him, with her face pressed into the muddy leaves of the forest. Her heart was beating so hard she thought it would explode out of her ears, and she writhed and twisted, trying to fight free.

His voice sounded in her ear again. "They said, *unspoiled*, but I have a mind to teach you a lesson."

"Dai." Another man spoke. "We don't have time for this."

Dai stiffened and sneered. "I don't have to answer to you, Madoc."

A pair of boots stopped beside Rhiann's nose. "But you do answer to me."

She knew that voice. It belonged to one of her father's captains, a man named Gruffydd.

Dai grunted as he reluctantly lifted himself off of Rhiann.

Before Rhiann could properly gather her legs under her for a second attempt at freedom, Gruffydd reached down, grasped her under her arms, and yanked her to her feet. He lifted her so high that her toes barely touched the ground and hauled her over to where the men's horses were tethered. He shoved Rhiann towards his horse, and she found herself caught in Madoc's arms.

This, by some miracle, was the same Madoc who'd been one of Cade's father's men and had helped them last night, little though his help had been. Madoc was a squat, bulky man, his shoulders broad from years of swordplay. Though his hair was gray, she was not going to underestimate his strength or endurance. His face was impassive as he gazed at her. Rhiann didn't know if his loyalty to the dead Cadwallon, or his disloyalty to her father, would stretch any further than it already had.

Madoc pulled Rhiann toward him so his face was only inches from hers. "You will stay close, and you will obey, or face the consequences. Do you understand?"

Rhiann nodded. *In the last twelve hours, I've burned the stables, freed Cade, escaped from Aberffraw, and swum the Menai Strait. I can wait my chance, if there is one.*

With Madoc's help, Gruffydd threw her across the withers of his horse, face down. She struggled for purchase to pull herself upright, but Gruffydd mounted behind her and pushed her down with his hand on the small of her back.

"You'll stay there where I can see you." Gruffydd gathered the reins and turned the horse's head.

Cade! Where are you? Even as Rhiann thought those words, she countered them with a frantic prayer that he wouldn't find himself captive again because of a foolish attempt to rescue her.

In close formation, the three horses came out of the forest and onto a wide road. The sky was gray all the way down to the ground, and the rain began falling harder now, or at least it seemed that way because they were out from under the trees. Rhiann rested her cheek on the horse's warm coat, feeling the rain drip down her face. She closed her eyes, choosing not to watch the cobbles fly past under the horse's hooves as Gruffydd picked up the pace. Because of its resemblance to the roads on Anglesey, she decided that this must be the Roman road that ran from Caerleon in the east to Caernarfon on the western coast.

The Romans had marched away from Britain over two hundred years before, leaving their roads and ruined forts behind them. The roads, many of which were still well-maintained, were the fastest pathways across Wales, but many of the forts had been abandoned. One lay at Caernarfon. The stones of another were underneath Aberffraw, and a third on the tip of Anglesey. Her father had allowed her to visit that ruin once, along with Alcfrith, in an attempt to bring his wife out of her impenetrable grief after the birth of yet another stillborn daughter.

Rhiann's neck ached fiercely with every yard as she bounced and shook on the trotting horse's bony shoulders. Fortunately, it wasn't long before they crested the last hill above the sea and saw the little village of Caernarfon laid out before them on the water's edge, half a mile away. Unfortunately, just discernable through the driving rain, were three Saxon longboats pulled up on the beach near the mouth of a river that emptied into the sea just to the south of the village.

The men with Rhiann checked their horses at the sight while Rhiann grew lightheaded at what this might mean. She pushed up with her arms, trying to throw herself backwards off the horse, while at the same time see the boats more clearly.

"Your father is as good as his word." A smile of satisfaction lit Gruffydd's face. "I will get paid today after all."

"Let me up," Rhiann said.

To her surprise, Gruffydd relented. He grasped her around the waist and effortlessly pulled her to a sitting position in front of him.

"You'll be warming a Saxon bed before the day is out," Dai said.

"Maybe more'n one," Gruffydd said, a smirk in his voice.

"How did you know they'd be here?" Real fear rose in Rhiann's chest, far greater than anything she had felt during her escape from Aberffraw or her swim across the Strait.

"They came first to Aberffraw, of course," Gruffydd said. "Your Saxon husband-to-be, Peada, sent word yesterday evening of their arrival, shortly before the feast began. When you up and left, your father sent us after you, with the idea that they would sail here to meet us to take possession of you."

"Weren't too pleased with your father to find you gone last night," Dai said. "Thought he meant to go back on his word."

Thwtt.

An arrow punched through Dai's leather armor and into his heart. He put a hand to his chest and touched the arrow point poking through his surcoat, and then looked at Rhiann. She met his eyes. It didn't seem possible that he could be dying right in front of her. Rhiann's breath caught in her throat, but Dai wasn't breathing. Slowly, he toppled off his horse.

"Cadwallon always had the devil's own luck!" Gruffydd said. "Damn him that his son is no different."

Gruffydd cursed again and swung his horse around to see Cade riding towards them down the slope from the Roman fort. Rhiann's heart lifted at the sight him. He hadn't abandoned her, just as he'd promised. She forced herself to focus on him instead of her fear, or Dai's death, trying not think of anything but that Cade was here, and he was trying to save her, even if he had to kill her father's men to do it.

Gruffydd reached for his sword, but this time Rhiann reacted more quickly than he. Her heart pounding in her ears, she jammed her elbow into Gruffydd's belly and clutched the hilt of his sword, determined to prevent him from drawing it. Gruffydd chose to grasp her around the waist and use her as a shield instead of pushing her hands aside, but his move came too late. Cade sent an arrow into the soft tissue below his collarbone.

"Christ in a cart!" Gruffydd's right arm hung useless, but his left still held Rhiann in a vice-like grip.

Cade came to a stop some thirty yards away—easy range for a man with a bow. He was too close for either Madoc or Gruffydd to get away, but far enough from them that he was out of the reach of a thrown knife. Madoc moved his horse farther from Gruffydd and Rhiann, trying to split Cade's attention. Cade already had a third arrow pressed into his bow and was directing Cadfan with his knees.

"Take your hand from your sword," Cade instructed Madoc, who obeyed, holding both hands above his head and letting his horse's reins fall free.

Gruffydd held Rhiann in front of him, his body stiff. "My lord. I would not have allowed her to come to harm."

Cade tipped his head towards the Saxons on the shore. "That looks like harm to me."

Gruffydd had no answer.

"Release Rhiannon," Cade said.

Gruffydd obeyed, lowering Rhiann to the ground with his good arm. She ran to Cadfan. Cade removed his own foot from the stirrup to allow her a leg up, and she scrambled onto the horse behind him.

"Did they harm you?" he said.

"No. I'm not hurt." Rhiann focused hard on breathing, trying to stop herself from gasping and to fight off the rushing in her ears. She bent her head forward and clutched the back of Cade's cloak. While Cade had suddenly become someone else—a dangerous soldier as opposed to the young man she'd been traveling with, and it made her a little afraid of him—she was much more frightened of Gruffydd and the Saxons.

"Please forgive me, my lord, and allow me to come with you," Madoc said. "It was I who spoke to you through the door last night."

"Shut it, traitor," Gruffydd said through gritted teeth.

Thwtt! Cade's arrow caught Gruffydd in the throat. His hands jerked up to grasp it, and then like Dai, he fell off his horse to the ground. The panicked horse raced away, followed by Dai's. Rhiann watched them go with regret, for they could have used another horse. An instant later, Cade had pulled a fourth arrow from his quiver and aimed it at Madoc, who cleared his throat.

"My lord. I served your father, and I would serve you."

"Where's Eben?" Rhiann said, suddenly remembering that there had been four men swimming in the Strait. "Did he turn back?"

"He's dead. Drowned," Madoc said.

Hysterical laughter bubbled up in Rhiann's chest, and she fought it down. She mustn't lose control and distract Cade, who had remained calm throughout. He now sat silent, studying Madoc. He made an odd motion with his head, almost like he was trying to physically dismiss a thought from his mind, and then he spoke. "Why should I not shoot you too?"

Madoc put out both hands, palms upwards in supplication. "I served Cadfael only because your mother gave him her allegiance. I had nowhere else to go. I am not innocent, true, but I was only doing my duty."

"Madoc did help me free you, Cade," Rhiann said. "Your mother obviously felt she could trust him."

Cade turned his head to the side, trying to see both Rhiann behind him and Madoc in front. "I don't know my mother, but I do know you. We still have some distance to ride before we reach Dinas Emrys. The terrain is difficult and the land potentially hostile as much of it remains in your father's hands. I could use another sword."

"He saved me from Dai's attentions too," Rhiann said.

Cade gave her a sharp look at that and then turned to Madoc. "You may come. I can use your arm if you will put it to my service."

Madoc dismounted at Cade's signal and walked to Cadfan, putting a hand on the horse's neck. Then he knelt. "I swore to serve your father until death, and I never broke that oath. I swear to serve you, my lord, in his stead." He looked up then, just a quick glance. It was only an instant before his eyes slid away, but it was time enough for Rhiann to see something in them that made her uncomfortable—something like desire, but not—something which she couldn't identify.

"I accept your fealty, Madoc," Cade said, unaware that Rhiann was having second thoughts. "Now rise and mount. Those Saxons are too close, and Cadfael may have planned other dangers for us between here and Dinas Emrys."

4

Cade

As Cade had feared, the Saxons were none too pleased about being denied their promised prize. He'd watched them from his vantage point at the Roman fort before shooting his first arrow at Rhiann's captors. For their part, the Saxons had seen the events on the ridge above the town and now, with some shouting and gesturing, had gathered themselves to take action. Four men had mounted and were headed inland.

"Let's go!" Madoc returned to his horse and turned its head towards the southeast.

Rhiann clutched Cade's waist as he spurred Cadfan after Madoc. "We can outrun them, can't we?"

"Maybe," Cade said. "Cadfan's tired and hungry; we all are."

As if to punctuate that statement, Rhiann's stomach growled and she pressed her hand to her belly. "My father locked me in my room with only bread and water for three days after I refused my first suitor. I can last out."

Cade's expression turned even more grim, aware as she was that she didn't have a choice, but also knowing, as perhaps she didn't, that there was a significant difference between sitting hungrily in one's room, staring out the window in righteous indignation after being misused by one's father, and riding half-way across Gwynedd without food.

"I'm sorry I made you wait to eat the apples," he said.

"Do you still have them?"

"You're sitting on them. After Madoc and the other men captured you, I set your horse free, but not before I transferred your saddle and bags to Cadfan. I would have kept your horse too, but I didn't want to be burdened with both animals, especially as I didn't know how far I'd have to go to find you."

Cade slowed Cadfan, who'd begun to labor under their combined weight, and checked the road behind. He couldn't see any Saxons, but that didn't mean they weren't there.

"We need to hide, not outrun them," Cade called to Madoc.

"They can't know the area well, my lord." Madoc shifted in his seat to look back at Rhiann and Cade. "They should soon give up."

"Not soon enough," Cade said under his breath to Rhiann. "Saxons never do."

They'd ridden a mile from the Roman fort when they reached the Seiont River. It circumscribed Caernarfon, and whether they'd taken the other road due south or this one, which ran southeast, they would have had to cross it. The river was running high from the all rain but looked passable.

"I was able to ford it a week ago," Cade told Madoc and Rhiann.

When Cade and his men had come this way from Dinas Emrys, they'd scouted up and down the bank, looking for a usable ford besides the one at the road, but there were none. Dangerous rapids flowed only a few yards upstream, and the river widened downstream, deepening as it made its way to the sea.

"Not again," Rhiann moaned from her seat behind Cade.

"It's not like you can get any wetter than you are now," Cade said. The rain dripped off the hood of his cloak and onto his face.

"I'll go across first," Madoc said. "No point getting the lady wet before she needs to be."

Cade nodded, and Madoc entered the water. He splashed his way across and up the other side.

"There's a dip in the middle you'll need to watch for," he said, "but if you skirt that rock, you should be fine."

Rhiann sighed. "All right; I'm ready," though she didn't sound it.

Cade urged Cadfan forward, trying to hurry but aware that one misstep might cause him to lose his footing and send all of them into the water. It took no time at all to cross. As they came up the opposite bank, Cade chanced a look back. Two of the four Saxon warriors were now in sight on the road behind them. Madoc noted them too.

"My lord!" he said in warning.

"I see them." Cade pulled his bow from its rest on his back. Cadfan danced sideways, responding to Cade's tension. Fortunately, Saxons are not archers as a rule, and these two were no exception.

"I need you to dismount, Rhiann, and hide," Cade said. "You're safer in the woods where they'll have to hunt to find you if they get past me."

"I understand, my lord." She slid to the ground.

Trusting that Rhiann would know enough to make herself secure, Cade pulled an arrow from his quiver, pressed it into the bow and loosed it. The first arrow took the lead rider's horse in the chest and the second went through the rider's own heart. The other Saxon checked his horse at the sight of what had happened to his companion. In the time it took Cade to press and loose another arrow, he flattened himself to his horse's neck so Cade didn't have an easy target. Cade's arrow caught the Saxon high in the shoulder. It was a hit that would slow him, but not stop him.

Rather than give Cade another chance, the Saxon pulled on the reins, urging his horse to change course, and head for the field to the left of the road. He was looking for shelter, but he wasn't going to find it soon enough to evade Cade. He was only a hundred yards from the ford now, easy shooting for a Welsh archer. Cade pressed another arrow, sure he could bring the man down, but then Madoc broke from his posting at Cade's side. He pushed his horse down the bank and into the river, his sword raised high.

Cade shook his head at the waste of energy and focused again on the Saxon, releasing his fourth arrow. It hit the Saxon's horse in the neck. The horse stumbled, and the Saxon leapt from his back. Madoc, meanwhile, covered the distance between the ford and the Saxon within a count of ten. The Saxon, with his sword arm useless and his horse down, didn't have a chance. Madoc launched himself at the Saxon, his hands going for his throat. The man feebly tried to fend him off, but the force of Madoc's leap was too much for him to counter, and he fell to the ground beneath the Welshman.

Madoc's horse blocked Cade's view of the two men, and Cade craned his neck to see beyond it. "What are you doing?"

Madoc didn't reply.

Cade knew he had shouted loud enough for Madoc to hear, even over the rushing of the river. Irritated with his own slowness, Cade finally admitted what his gut already knew. He cursed himself for not heeding his instincts about Madoc from the first. His only excuse was that the rain had dulled his senses at their initial meeting and he'd been distracted by Rhiann. "We don't have time for this!"

Madoc still didn't answer, but his horse shifted, revealing Madoc's form bent over the body of the Saxon. Blood had seeped from the man's wounds onto the ground. Then, Madoc straightened, wiped the back of a hand across his mouth, and began to paw through the Saxon's clothing. He pulled a sack from the man's waist, along with his belt knife. Stuffing the items into his saddlebags, Madoc hauled himself into the saddle and rode back to Cade. He splashed across the ford and up the bank.

Cade studied Madoc as he reached him, although Madoc didn't meet his gaze. Instead, he pulled the Saxon's pouch from his scrip and handed it to Cade.

"I was gathering evidence, my lord," he said.

"Of what?"

"King Cadfael's bargain," he said. "If you are to press your claim to the throne of Gwynedd, some Saxon artifacts may strengthen your case before the Council and confirm Cadfael's treachery."

"I plan to take the throne over Cadfael's dead body," Cade said. "Between you and Rhiann, we have witnesses enough to Cadfael's plans. Still, I grant your point."

Madoc looked relieved, and Cade didn't press him, willing to defer the moment when he'd have to confront the man. Now, Cade turned Cadfan and headed up the trail to a likely spot where Rhiann might have entered the woods. "Rhiann!"

"I'm here, Cade." She dropped from the branch of a tree growing a dozen feet into the woods. She was even grimier than before. Leaves had caught in her hair, which had come loose from its braid. Dirt smudged her forehead and cheek and coated her already wet clothing. To Cade, she appeared more beautiful than ever.

"Come quickly," he said. "We've killed two of the Saxons, but we don't know where the others are. They could have taken the second road from Caernarfon or backtracked to find us here."

"How long do you think they'll look for us?" she said.

Without second-guessing the impulse to touch her, Cade leaned down to give her his arm so she could mount Cadfan. She grasped his forearm, and he pulled her up behind him, before urging the horse up the road. "Either they'll find their dead friends and it will enrage them so they'll pursue us for hours, or they'll cut their losses and give up. I'd prefer to get as far away from here as possible to a place where they will no longer be our concern."

They rode a mile without speaking, the only sound the clopping of the horses' hooves and the rain on their hoods. Then Rhiann said, "Can I have an apple? It's all I can think of."

"Of course," Cade said.

Rhiann rummaged in the saddle bag and came out with two apples. She turned to Madoc and held one out to him but he shook his head.

"Save them for yourself, Lady Rhiann," he said. "I'm not hungry now."

Cade shook his head too when Rhiann offered one to him. She shrugged, took a big bite, and gave a huge sigh. Then she leaned her forehead into Cade's back between his shoulder blades. He couldn't suppress a smile at her obvious contentment, even as he trembled at her closeness. He had touched her, and she him, a dozen times since they'd met. Already it was almost a habit, but one Cade knew he couldn't get used to. The deep well of dangerous energy at his center—the power that he fought with all his strength—wasn't going to go away.

"How far do we have to go?" Rhiann took another bite. She'd already finished off one of the apples and, after tossing the first core into the woods, started in on the second.

"Fifteen miles," Cade said.

"How close by were you when Dai captured me?"

"Close enough," Cade said. "I was on my way back to you, having seen no one, when I heard your call. I trailed you onto the Roman road and then took a path to the east—a shortcut that brought me into Caernarfon more quickly than by the road. By then, I knew there were only three of them. I would not have let your father's men harm you, but I needed to know how many I faced before I showed myself."

"I know," she said, "but I was scared."

"I would that you were never scared again," Cade said, "but I cannot promise it."

Rhiann hugged Cade around the waist, still resting against him. "I've seen men die before, but never like that; never right in front of me."

His jaw was tight with the effort it took to control himself—and the thought of how close she'd come to real harm. Cade pressed his hand to hers. "The priest tells me *thou shalt not kill* and yet I've already killed more men in my life than I care to remember. And I will kill many more."

* * * * *

Cade didn't dare let his attention falter, not even for a moment. They were far closer now to Dinas Emrys than to Caernarfon, but they were riding through some of the most rugged country in Wales, and he had a sleeping girl in his arms. Rhiann had fallen asleep behind him, her head resting on his back. When her arms loosened, he'd pulled her in front of him before she could fall off Cadfan's back.

Cade supported her against his chest with one arm around her while his other hand held the reins. A stray breeze lifted a lock of her hair and swept it across his face. She smelled so sweet—of faith and innocence—and he longed to stay just as they were: her asleep and him her gallant protector. But it couldn't last.

The rain had stopped an hour earlier. They'd finally ridden high enough to rise above the fog that had drifted in to obscure everything beyond a dozen yards on any side. Cade looked west, towards the ocean. He could see nothing but a thick layer of white below them, merging with the gray sea and sky. Good. The Saxons would have returned to their boats.

Cade had allowed Madoc to ride ahead of him so he could keep an eye on the man. Madoc claimed to have ridden this road in Cadwallon's company many a time, and more recently with Cadfael. Cade contemplated Madoc's straight back and soldierly bearing. Madoc's left hand drifted to the hilt of his sword as if reassuring himself of its presence. Cade was going to have to deal with Madoc when they stopped, which was going to be sooner than he liked. The sun would set in an hour, and Cade couldn't risk bringing Madoc into Dinas Emrys.

Slowly they picked their way up one hill, down another, around a third, and up again. Yr Wyddfa (Mt. Snowdon) loomed closer and higher above them with every step, her peaks decorated with snow, even this close to spring.

Madoc spoke, breaking the long silence between them. "I was there, you know, when Cadfael cut your father down. It was I who delivered word of his death to your mother."

Cade focused again on Madoc's back, thunderstruck, and tried to marshal his thoughts to make a sensible reply. "You told my mother that Cadfael killed my father?" *Why does he confess this? To invite my confidence?*

Madoc glanced back, his face completely blank, and then turned forward again. "Of course not. I didn't see it happen. It didn't seem anyone did right at the time. I was simply the messenger."

As Madoc spoke, Cade let himself fall farther behind. It wasn't so much what Madoc said that bothered him, but how he said it. Every sentence appeared to have deeper meanings beyond the obvious ones, and his words were accompanied by a sneer, a wink, or a stare Cade couldn't quite interpret.

"I didn't know what Cadfael had done, then. Nobody did. I told your mother that Cadwallon had died, borne to the ground by the Saxon menace. It was only later that the rumors started." He glanced again at Cade, who nodded.

"I've heard the rumors," Cade said.

"Your father, Cadwallon, was as fine a fighter king as Wales has ever seen. He defeated three Saxon kings in his day." Madoc held up a hand to show the significance of the number.

"Unfortunately, he couldn't defeat that last man, who wasn't even a Saxon," Cade said.

"That's right."

"So my mother didn't know the truth when she married Cadfael?"

"No, she didn't," Madoc said.

Cade's foster father had tried to tell him that more than once, the last time not long ago. Cade hadn't truly believed him. Suddenly, with the reality of Rhiann in his arms, much like the girl his mother must have been at the time, some of the anger and confusion he'd felt towards her all his life eased. It was replaced, just a little, by pity. Cade looked down at Rhiann, her eyes closed in sleep. *I had a mother who loved me enough to give me away, and a second one who loved me as much as her own son. Who had Rhiann had? No one. And yet, she'd been strong enough to risk her life for me.*

The horses came around a hill and the path crossed through a small clearing. Cade made an instant decision. "We'll stop here."

"It's not night yet!" Madoc said.

Cade shook his head. "Dinas Emrys is still too far away to reach before dark." He spoke the truth, though not all of it.

Madoc didn't argue further, just stared up at the fort that loomed far above them. A ray of light pierced the heavy cloud cover and struck the uppermost tower. Cade moved Cadfan to stand beside Madoc and looked with him.

Madoc tipped his chin, gesturing at the fort on its hill. "You fly the Dragon banner above the towers. It's been a long time since anyone has flown that flag in Gwynedd."

"It was my father's flag, and his father's. Soon the red dragon will fly above all the fortresses in Wales, even Aberffraw."

"Long ago, dragons lived beneath Dinas Emrys," Madoc said, and then began to chant the words of the prophecy. Although the words themselves were reverent, his tone was less so, on the edge of mocking:

"Two dragons are they
One red, of our people
One white, of our enemies,

Who lord over us from sea to sea.
But soon one shall come.
He shall raise us up
And drive all our enemies away."

"So the bards sing of Dinas Emrys," Cade said, taking the poem as Taliesin had sung it, not in the way Madoc might have meant. "Why do you think it was the first fort I took from Cadfael?"

"You took it from Cadfael, yet you disbelieve that you are the one foretold in the prophecies?" Madoc said. "Taliesin spoke those words of you."

"Taliesin is gone," Cade said. "He may have come for me once, but he is long dead, and there is no one left to take his place. We fight now without his help, and I am not so full of my own self as to think that any prophecy he may have left was meant for me. I know who I am." *Or what I am.*

Cade had had enough of Madoc. He dismounted, carefully pulling Rhiann down with him. He carried her to a grassy spot to lay her down. She opened her eyes and lifted her head to look at him.

"Shush. Sleep." He kissed her forehead, and she lay back, instantly asleep again. Cade turned to face Madoc, his hands on his hips.

Madoc dismounted to match him, and they both paused. Madoc tipped his head to one side. "Aahh. I was afraid of this. I thought perhaps you were saving the girl for later, but that isn't it at all, is it? My help with the Saxons did not convince you of my worth?"

"You helped yourself to that Saxon, as I recall," Cade said. "I don't know how you've kept your secret from your fellow men-at-arms."

"I am fortunate in that I've been allowed to keep my human shape," Madoc said. "Most men see what they want to see. Nothing more; nothing less."

Cade nodded, understanding as only he could. "I'm not most men. How long did you wait before telling Cadfael of my escape?"

Madoc's eyes lit with an inner mirth, and he dropped any attempt to lull Cade into complacency. "I gave you a head start."

"You have arisen from the Underworld," Cade said. "I know your kind."

"And I know you," Madoc said.

Cade tipped his head to one side, finding a small smile hovering at the corner of his lips, despite the danger inherent in this confrontation. "Perhaps. The next move is up to you. I'm not in a killing mood at the moment, so if you wish, I'll allow you to turn around and walk away. Whatever you do, however, I warn you not to touch the girl."

Madoc smiled again, this time like a cat who had just finished a bowl of cream. "That Saxon was most obliging. I don't need the girl, though she would be tasty. You, on the other hand, look quite thin—even, shall I say, pale?"

"It's different for me," Cade said.

"Is it? How?"

Cade pulled his sword from its sheath. It was the first time he'd held it, and a thrill shot through him as he wielded it. Then he felt the power surge within him, so much so he was afraid he couldn't contain it. He didn't have time to question how or why, or what had changed in him when he grasped the sword. "I'm not evil."

Madoc laughed. "You wouldn't be, would you, if the prophecies are true. For myself, I gave up thinking in those terms long ago." He drew his own sword to counter Cade's.

Cade raised his sword high, ready to strike, but then a stick cracked in the woods. Madoc and Cade looked at each other, instantly frozen. "Tell me right now if they're with you," Cade said.

"No," Madoc said. "It's the Saxons, perhaps?"

Cade lowered his sword as well as his profile by crouching down. Madoc didn't bother, sure of his own invincibility. In unison, the two men turned toward the place from which they'd heard the sound come, scanning the trees for whatever or whoever dared to approach them.

Thwtt.

An arrow appeared in Madoc's left shoulder. He staggered to one knee, and Cade dove face down, not willing to risk even the slight damage an arrow could cause him, not with Rhiann to protect.

"By Cunedda's arse!" Madoc ripped the arrow from his shoulder and threw himself flat to the ground. "I thought Saxons weren't archers."

Cade didn't bother to reply. On his stomach, he crept forward. He could sense the fear coursing through the veins of the men ahead of him, drawing him to them like a beacon. He reached the edge of the trees and stopped, listening hard. Very slowly, he stood and then moved on silent feet toward their attackers, who, after all, couldn't be very far back into the trees if they'd been able to see well enough to shoot at Madoc.

Cade felt the man before he saw him. He was unmistakably Saxon, evident by the shape of his helmet and his lack of proper armor. His small bow—far smaller than the Welsh longbows—was drawn, but he jerked it from left to right in quick, uneven movements. He was afraid. He had a right to be, although he couldn't know the full extent of why.

Cade moved forward, finding that he had never felt the power within him as he did in that moment; that if anyone could see him, they couldn't help but know it too. The power was difficult to control in the best of times. Holding this sword Rhiann had found for him was like riding an unbroken horse. It worried Cade. Resolved to do without the weapon, he thrust it into his sheath, forcing himself to rein in his power for these last few moments, else he lose control of himself and his surroundings.

Still turned away, the Saxon never saw him coming. Cade came up behind him and stifled the Saxon's cry with his right hand whilst wrapping his left arm around his shoulders. The Saxon froze at his touch. Cade closed his eyes, finally allowing the wave to rush through him, as if a waterfall was precipitating from the top of his head and falling through him to his feet. Relief flooded his senses, bringing him almost to the point of tears. He shone from within, power pouring from his fingertips with a white light that Madoc had mistaken for weakness.

As the Saxon died, Cade's body strengthened. Madoc had not been wrong that he was hungry—but not for what Madoc hungered. Madoc was a demon from the Underworld, undead and without a soul, feasting on the flesh and blood of humans. Cade possessed the power of the *sidhe* themselves, even if in the end he was a charlatan, carrying their gift inside him but never becoming one of them. Most of the time, he could control that power, right to the point where it burst from him, overwhelming whatever hapless creature found himself within his grasp.

Cade stepped back. The man he'd killed stood straight and unmoving, and then slowly toppled over, like a tree falling to earth. He would never move again. With a sigh, Cade turned aside, intending to return to the clearing and kill the remaining Saxons before disposing of Madoc. He'd gone only three steps, however, when he nearly bumped into Rhiann, who stood rooted to the ground much like the Saxon had been, her face whiter than Cade's. Although Cade was stronger when he released the *sidhe*-creature within him, at the sight of Rhiann, he pulled the power back inside himself, like suppressing a flame with a quick pinch of his fingers. Even so, it was too late. She had seen him—seen him as he really was.

Rhiann took a step back, tears coursing down her cheeks. She shook her head. "No, no, no!"

She stumbled on a hidden root. Cade reached out a hand to stop her from falling, but she shrieked, recovered her balance, and ran from him. He watched her go for half a heartbeat, not that he had one, and ran his fingers through his hair. He couldn't let her run away. Somehow, he'd have to make her understand.

Cade took one long stride after her, and then another.

5

Rhiann

Rhiann ran from him, her heart pounding so loudly in her ears she couldn't hear Cade behind her; didn't know if he was chasing her and almost didn't care. She skirted the clearing where Madoc battled with two other men, their weapons ringing out, metal on metal, as they clashed. She had run from Madoc initially, having woken at his curse and seen him yank the arrow from his shoulder, his face transfigured into something hideous, something that she'd only imagined in her worst nightmares.

There were stories, of course. Who hadn't been riveted by the tales told by older boys, trying to scare the younger ones with monsters and demons, undead creatures who ripped the souls from their prey, even as they devoured their bodies? But they were just stories, all the children knew. Except they weren't.

Rhiann couldn't believe it. She'd seen the power of the gods flowing through Cade, an inner light illuminating him, as he killed that man. Never had she imagined anything like it. Even in the midst of her worst nightmares, she'd never believed those faery stories could be true.

Cade caught her three steps into the woods on the opposite side of the clearing. His arm clamped around her waist. She drew breath to scream, but he clapped a hand over her mouth and pulled her tight against his body.

"I will not hurt you," he said.

Rhiann tried to get her teeth around one of his fingers like she'd done to Dai, but Cade covered her nose as well as her mouth and spoke in her ear again.

"Don't do it. You know what I am, but you also know that I have not harmed you up until now. You can trust me."

Rhiann fought briefly, reason warring with emotion and losing, and then sagged against him, out of air as he knew she would be. He relaxed his hand. Rhiann took in a shaky breath.

"I saw what you did." She turned within the circle of his arm. "I saw what you are!"

"And you've been given a glimpse into the real world in which we live," Cade said. "The one I fight to save you from seeing every day of my life."

"You're a—" Rhiann stopped, taking in another shaky breath. But Cade's head was turned from her, looking through the trees to the men still fighting in the clearing. Madoc must have defeated one of his opponents, for only he and one Saxon remained upright. Night had fallen, and all Rhiann could see were dim shapes beyond the trees. In truth, Cade was all she could see. He assaulted her senses, confused them, and forced her to face what couldn't be true.

"I'm a ... what?" Cade said, still watching Madoc.

"You're a demon," she said. "One without a soul, an ellyllon."

"An elf?" He looked down at her, amusement showing at what she'd called him. "Next thing you'll be calling me a pixie." He lifted her chin with one finger and then dropped his hand after only a brief touch as if her skin might burn him. "Are you so sure you know what I am?"

"You killed that man," Rhiann said.

"That I did. And in a most unearthly fashion. Yet, I know, as you do not, that I stand at the crossroads of Annwn. In one direction lie the demons from the Underworld, waiting to loose themselves upon us. On the other are the free people of Wales."

Words came back to her, ones that Taliesin had once spoken. The court bard had sung them in her father's hall, much to Cadfael's disgust at the time. Rhiann said:

"Cadwaladr is a spear at the side of his men.

In the forest, in the field, in the vale, on the hill,

Cadwaladr is a candle in the darkness walking with
us.

Gloriously he will come and the Cymry will rise ..."

"You are the second person to quote prophecy at me tonight," Cade said. "I find it no more compelling now than before."

Rhiann found herself trembling, and Cade released her. It was so unexpected, she staggered, but he didn't catch her. He was already turning away. He removed an arrow from the quiver at his back, one of three that remained, and walked out from under the trees. Madoc knelt on the ground, his hands resting on his knees, a sword rammed through his midsection. The sword point stuck out of the leather armor at Madoc's back. The man Madoc had fought was on the ground, dead.

Rhiann moved closer, following Cade despite her fears.

Madoc turned to look as Cade approached. "Help me remove it. It's at a bloody awkward angle."

Cade walked up to him and put his left hand on the handle of the sword. The other still held the arrow, fisted in his right hand. He raised it above his head and said, "No."

"My lord!" Madoc's voiced went high. "I'm one of you!"

Cade brought the arrow down with terrific force, stabbing Madoc through the heart. "No, you're not."

Madoc gasped and collapsed, falling sideways to the earth. Cade stepped back and then looked over at Rhiann. Like a puppet on strings, she moved towards him out of the trees. At that moment, the clouds parted, and the moon shown brightly down. Cade looked so normal beneath it, as if he were no more than a young man her own age and not the otherworldly creature she'd seen him become. Maybe he was both.

"Why did you do that?" Rhiann said, her voice barely a whisper.

"He was a demon, one who was once a man but returned to the land of the living. In the last two years, I've sent countless beings like him back to the Underworld."

Rhiann's eyes tracked from Cade's face, still glowing in the moonlight, to the prone form of Madoc. "Why do you say you are not like him?"

"I don't serve Arawn," Cade said. "I've made no bargain with the Underworld."

"No bargain?" Rhiann glanced at Madoc again and then shied away. "You mean—?"

Cade's chest rose and fell once, and then stilled. He'd forced the air out of himself, and it came to her that she'd known all along that something was wrong about the way he breathed. Or didn't breathe. Rhiann thought back to their flight from Aberffraw. As she'd sat behind him on Cadfan, she'd never taken note of his breathing, but she realized now that normally his chest never rose and fell at all.

"Two years ago, a snowstorm caught me by surprise while I was hunting in the mountains near Bryn y Castell. I became thoroughly lost. I was desperate to save myself, but each passing hour diminished my hope for survival. Then suddenly, the snow swirled upwards long enough for me to spy an owl sitting before me, resting on a fallen tree trunk. It flew up into the air as if inviting me to follow it. So I did. The owl led me to a cave. Sure that the Christ had saved me, I lit a fire to warm myself. I thought I was alone there, but then a woman appeared out of the darkness at the back of the cave. She said she'd been waiting for me for a very long time.

"I didn't know her; didn't even believe her. When I stood to greet her, she moved so fast I could hardly credit it. One moment she was ten yards away, and the next she had pressed her lips to mine. Her touch paralyzed me. I fell unconscious. When I awoke, I was as you find me now, and she was gone."

"Who was this woman?" Rhiann said. "The tales of the *sidhe* are many, but not here, not like this, not—" She broke off, remembering the days she'd run with the peasant and craft-workers' children until her father had put a stop to it. On rainy afternoons, they would hide in the loft above the stables, the air heady with the smell of new-mown hay, while Rhys, the most gifted story-teller, would regale the other children with tales he swore were true.

Again Cade's breathless sigh. "Do you know of the legend of Arianrhod?"

"Oh," Rhiann breathed. "I do. She's the keeper of death; the ruling aspect of the triple goddess: mother, maiden, crone. In her hands spins the silver wheel of life and death, and into her possession fall all men's souls."

"I don't know about all men's," Cade said, "but certainly mine."

"As the crone, Cerridwen, she is the devouring goddess who kills and eats her prey and then births him again. But why—" Rhiann stopped again, unable to voice her question. Cade seemed to know what she was asking.

"Why did she choose me? Why did she give me the power of the *sidhe* without the understanding or strength to bear it?" Cade barked a laugh, although there was no amusement in him. "Or better yet, why didn't she make me a demon like Madoc here. I could prey upon my victims without grief or remorse, reveling in the joy of it without the guilt." He kicked Madoc's body with the toe of his boot and then tipped his head to gaze at the stars above them. "Believe me, I would dearly love to see Arianrhod again so I could ask her."

Rhiann's head was spinning, trying to absorb Cade's words and reconcile the young man before her with the deadly power he wielded. "So you are *sidhe* as she is?"

"Yes," Cade said. "And no. Whatever I am, I am not a god. Even without my soul, I live in this world, not in theirs."

"But the way you looked when you killed that man!" Rhiann's voice rose as her anxiety returned in full force, and the questions multiplied inside her head. "You didn't even need to use your sword!"

"I can kill with a touch," Cade said. "But at the same time, I kill when I touch. That is both the benefit, and the cost, of immortality."

"You've touched me," Rhiann said, aghast, finally recognizing the truth in what she had seen. "You didn't kill me. Why?"

"I cannot even describe to you the control it took to spare you," Cade said. "No man or beast is safe from me, even when I would prefer not to kill at all."

Cade turned away from Rhiann. In a swift motion, he pulled his sword from his sheath and raised it above his head. The glow from the moon met its point in a flash of light like a falling star, and then Cade struck Madoc's silent form. The blow severed the head from the body, and it rolled away. Rhiann watched, choking on her horror. She gazed at Cade, unable to look away. He loomed over her in the moonlight. Then his shoulders sagged, he sheathed his sword, and her sense of him diminished.

Cade spoke again. "You ask me why? Because the gods play us for fools." He turned on his heel, walking away from the dead men on the ground and towards Cadfan. The horse quietly cropped the grass, no longer upset by the carnage, although he'd been frightened earlier. Perhaps he'd seen too many such scenes before.

Rhiann wasn't done with her questions and hurried to catch up. "And yet you wear a piece of the True Cross." She stopped beside Cade and pointed to the fragment resting on his chest, strung on a fine chain around his neck.

"I wear it as a reminder of who I am," he said. "Who I want to be."

"Maybe to be a candle in the darkness, you must be able to see without one," she said.

Cade stared at Rhiann—stared through her, even. "You give me hope." He very carefully placed both hands on her shoulders. That he would touch her on purpose shocked her, as her innocent touch had perhaps shocked him, and testified to how serious he was. Cade bent down so his eyes were level with Rhiann's. "I swear to you, that I will never hurt you."

Cadwaladr, the promised battle leader, was *sidhe*, a creature of the hidden places who'd risen whole out of legend to walk among his people. And yet, because of that, Rhiann believed him.

* * * * *

I tap, tap, tap my way up the long winding road to Dinas Emrys. Night is falling, and I stumble on unseen stones. My back is bent with age and the burden of my pack, but still, I have the strength for this task. Even as I ascend to the crest of the hill, my pace quickens, vitality returning to my arms and legs.

It has been so long since I've been here; so many, many years of wandering, I can't quite pinpoint the last time I strode through its doors. Was it in the reign of Arthur? Rhun? Cadwallon?

So many years ...

Moonlight streamed through the open window, making a pattern on the floor and dancing among the bodies of the sleeping women who lay around Rhiann. Three days had passed since she and Cade had arrived and she still slept restlessly, waking repeatedly in the night, every night, afraid she was disturbing the other women. It was Cade's fault, undoubtedly. For this night, she'd found a spot in a corner, far from the door.

The dream wasn't fading like most dreams, but hanging in front of her eyes like a ghostly tapestry. Now, she rolled onto her back to contemplate the rafters. She could be in any room, in any fort in Wales—even the very chamber where her father had imprisoned Cade. Trying to shake off the uncomfortable feeling the dream had given her, she sat up and surveyed the room. Before midnight, it must be, given the position of the moon.

Rhiann and Cade had arrived just before dawn at Dinas Emrys, the morning after Cade killed Madoc. Cade, with his otherworldly night vision, had led them unerringly up the steep road to the fort. Neither of them had wanted to camp at the clearing: Rhiann, because of the dead men and her thoughts, and Cade, because his power waned as the hour approached noon, and waxed to its greatest peak in the midnight hour. Even if he walked the earth like a normal man, like the *sidhe* themselves, he was trapped in the world of mist and shadows.

Cade. *Is he a demon or a god? Or does he fulfill the prophecies in some manner we can't determine now from where we sit? And does it matter? Under the moonlight in the clearing, he drew me to him like a fly to amber and held me fast. I didn't run again; I went with him without question, or without enough doubt to fear him as all reason said I should.*

To say Rhiann was unsettled was an understatement. She rubbed the sleep from her eyes, trying to push away the thoughts that wouldn't leave, and finally got to her feet. She tiptoed to the curtain that served as a door, separating the chamber from the upstairs hall. Ducking through it, she headed down the stairs to the great hall below and then on through it to the great front door. It was open a crack. Hoping not to wake the sleeping men who sprawled on the floor, on the tables, or even underneath them, she slipped out and moved down the steps to the courtyard.

It was a clear night but not cold, the aftermath of recent rain. The moon was even fuller and brighter than during the last night of their journey from Aberffraw. Stars speckled the sky like the freckles across her nose. It was as beautiful a night as Rhiann could imagine in Wales.

Breathing deeply, she strolled across the nearly empty courtyard, nodding to a guard who stood at the base of the wooden gate. She turned and mounted the steps to the battlements. As Cade had pointed out to her when they'd come through the gate that first morning, Dinas Emrys was built in stone. Pride had filled his voice at his father's vision.

Once on the heights, nearly twenty feet from the ground, she stopped. A young man sat sprawled before her, his back braced against the wall and his feet splayed out in front of him. He was awake. Without appearing to stare at him, Rhiann took note of his patched cloak, well-worn boots, and ancient satchel.

"Bracing isn't it?" he asked Rhiann, tipping his head to look into her face.

"The night?" She glanced up at the banner on the tower, silhouetted against the moon. "It is beautiful."

"No, to be alive!" With those words, he sprang to his feet, startling Rhiann into taking a step backwards. Now that he was upright, he towered over her, his shock of white-blonde hair sticking up in all directions and adding another two inches to his height. He was so thin, however, scrawny even, that she feared he might blow right off the battlements in the first, heavy wind.

"Who are you?" The words just came out, even as Rhiann realized they were rude, but couldn't take them back.

"You can call me Taliesin," he said. "I've come to see the high king."

"But Taliesin died—" Rhiann stopped, cutting off the words as Taliesin gazed at her, an expression on his face that was both quizzical and amused. She tried again. "There's no high king here. Not for a long time. There's Rhun who will rule at Bryn y Castell now that his father is dead, and Cadwaladr, who should be king in Gwynedd."

Taliesin began to chant:

"A warrior on a swift horse rides through the night,
He leaves turmoil in his wake.
With treachery afoot, he renews our faith
And brings to the Cymry a new Eden."

"That's—" Rhiann stopped.

"Quite wonderful, isn't it? I just made it up." Taliesin hummed a tune and appeared to dance a little jig, his hands on the stones of the rampart, supporting his weight.

Rhiann backed away farther, more uncertain than ever.

Taliesin gave her a pitying look. "Daughter of the usurper, what path do you hope to tread?"

"I—" Rhiann found herself stuttering again. "How do you know who I am?"

"You see what I see," Taliesin said. "You just don't know it yet."

Rhiann shook her head. His enigmatic sentences had created a fog in her mind. "I can bring you to Cadwaladr, if he's not asleep." She gestured below them to the courtyard.

"I accept your offer." Taliesin smiled and hoisted his pack over one shoulder. "Lead on."

Taliesin followed Rhiann down the stairs and across the courtyard to the keep. She pulled the great door open but as they crossed the threshold, Taliesin passed Rhiann in one stride. He paced down the great hall as if he owned the fort, heading towards Cade and Rhun, who now sat upon the dais at the far end. They hadn't been there before when Rhiann had crossed in the other direction.

"My lords!" Taliesin's voice echoed among the stones. "Greetings from Bryn y Castell."

Cade and Rhun stood in unison. "What is your message?" Rhun said. "You have word from Geraint?"

"Grim news, my lords, and urgent." Taliesin sounded so completely unlike the man Rhiann had met on the battlements, she could hardly believe he was the same person. Gone were the strange looks and grins, the clownish jigs and enigmatic tunes. Replacing the jester was a man of power, whose shadow rose over Cade and Rhun as he approached them. "I am Taliesin. I bring you word from Lord Morgan of Powys—of warriors coming west and north into Wales."

"Saxons?" Rhun said.

"Yes," Taliesin said, "but not Mercians. These are southerners, from Wessex."

"Which seeks to challenge both Penda and his Welsh allies." Rhun nodded his understanding. "I would not have thought that challenge would come so far west."

Cade turned to Rhun. "That region of Wales has been in chaos since the death of Eluedd of Powys. Morgan's control is tenuous at best. He will not have the strength to hold off an army of Saxons, in addition to his other challengers."

"Where does Lord Geraint hope to meet Morgan and his men?" Rhun asked Taliesin.

"At Caersws, before the Saxons can cross the Severn River," Taliesin said. "He intends to confront them in three days' time, with or without you."

"If we ride now, we will have time to travel to Bryn y Castell and then south after Geraint," Cade said. "The Saxons cannot be allowed to reach Gwynedd."

"Tonight," Rhun said. "I will order the men to ready themselves to leave, if you will lead us."

He strode off the dais, heading down the hall towards the spot where Rhiann stood. He was a bear of a man, far broader than Cade, although not as tall. He passed her and exited the hall without even a glance. She had no need to wonder why. She'd been at Dinas Emrys for three days, and he had yet to speak to her beyond his initial, very formal greeting. It was as Taliesin had implied: she was tainted with the stain of being her father's daughter, even though she had rescued Cade from Aberffraw.

Taliesin and Cade still stood at the end of the room, looking at each other in silent communication. Rhiann walked forward to stand beside Cade, but he ignored her too, although not for the same reason as Rhun.

"A man bearing your name took me from my mother's arms," Cade said to Taliesin.

Taliesin studied him. "I know it. It is the same wisdom that brings me here to you now."

"You hope to advise me, like—" Cade paused, clearly unable to say, *like he did*, or worse, *like you did my father*. Instead, he amended, "like the philosophers of old?"

"I offer you my services," Taliesin said. "All of them."

Cade didn't stammer as Rhiann had in the face of Taliesin's strangeness, just nodded. "I obviously have need of advice. Rhiann here could have told me not to enter the lion's den at Aberffraw. I was foolish."

"Not foolish," Taliesin corrected. "Naïve."

"It amounts to the same thing," Cade said.

Taliesin looked as if he disagreed, but Cade turned to Rhiann before he could say more. "You will stay here."

"No, I won't," Rhiann said. Cade blinked twice, and she kept talking. "I've spent my life in the shadows. I refuse to return to them now after only a few days in the light."

"I can promise you only darkness," Cade said.

Rhiann shook her head. "So you say, but that's not all I see."

"You no longer believe I am a danger to you?" he said.

"Not to me. I don't know what I think of you, but I believe that you won't hurt me." Rhiann lowered her voice so it didn't carry. "How many know what you are, beyond the few of us here? I would stay beside you if you would have me."

"Can you sing, Rhiannon of the raven hair?" Taliesin said, the jester of earlier peeking through the façade of counselor he'd donned for Cade.

"I can sing." Rhiann turned to him. "I can patch wounded men; I can pray over the dead. Anything but serve a father who doesn't deserve my loyalty, or that of any man."

"Your father is not here," Taliesin said. "Or perhaps, he is. It's up to you to decide if you are to let him into your house or leave him to shiver outside in the cold." He tipped his head to Cade. "Both of you."

"You speak in riddles, Taliesin," Cade said. "You always have."

"Taxes! Taxes!" Taliesin sang. *"Their taxes will lead to their death. The wise ruler bides his time before striking, defeating those who tax us."*

Cade turned to Rhiann, rolling his eyes at Taliesin's words. "The Taliesin of old may have prophesied that of me, and the son of Cadwallon I may be, but taxes are the lifeblood of any realm. No king can rule without them."

Taliesin sobered, his eyes intent on Cade's face. "Not all prophecy comes true. Without the prophecy, would the man still act? Or does the prophecy determine the action? Only one who knows himself can answer that."

"I know myself," Cade said. "We ride through the night for Bryn y Castell."

6

Cade

"You know what I am?" Cade said, his hands on his hips.

Taliesin and Cade were alone. Rhun had gone to organize the men, and Cade had sent Rhiann after him, telling her to find a bow and to practice shooting it. Cade was suddenly so angry with Taliesin —and the old man he'd once been, if such a thing were even possible—he felt his eyes glowing.

Taliesin, however, remained unconcerned. "Do you think you can shoot daggers to my heart?" He reclined in a chair and put his feet on the table. Then, pulling his belt knife from his waist, he began trimming his nails. "I dreamt of you—the last Pendragon."

"I am so sick of dreams and visions and prophecies." Cade spun on his heel and kicked one of the logs, which had rolled out of the fire, back into it. "I'd believe this was all a dream if it weren't so bloody real."

"The girl seems to think well of you, despite your—" Taliesin waved the knife in the air, "affliction."

"That's what it is too," Cade said. "It's as if I have a disease; not unlike when the healer told old Aeron that he had a growth inside him from which he would never recover. Gradually, Aeron was able to do less and less as it grew larger. One day it took his life."

"In you, however, it seems to have the opposite effect," Taliesin said.

"I grow in power. My senses strengthen, and yet—"

Taliesin looked up from his nails, studying Cade closely. "And yet you fear you lose more of your human self each day. You fear that given time, the changes within you will overtake you, and your true self will die."

"Oh, Christ." Cade pulled out a chair from beside Taliesin and dropped into it. "That's exactly it."

"I'm not saying it can't happen," Taliesin said, still in the same conversational tone, "but it seems to me it is up to you to decide if it does or not."

"You really think I have that choice?" Cade rubbed his eyes with his fingers, pushing back an imaginary headache. "When the power is upon me, I appear as an angel might, but I have more in common with the demons I'm fighting."

"Is your basic nature to be good or evil?" Taliesin said. "That, to me, is the essence of the issue."

"The priests tell us that all people are essentially evil," Cade said. "They say that only through belief in the Christ can we be good."

"Oh, well," Taliesin said, "that's easy then. If that's true, then you're no different from everyone else. Believe in Christ, and all your worries are over."

Cade glanced at him, wary. The sarcasm in his voice was unmistakable, but there was a kernel of truth in what he said. "I do believe in the Christ. The priests say—"

Taliesin didn't wait for him to finish, leaning forward and dropping his feet to the wooden floor with a thud. "I wasn't asking what the priests thought. I wanted to know what was in your heart."

"I have a choice," Cade said.

"Right." Taliesin put away his knife and rose to his feet. "That's all we need to know, then, isn't it?"

Cade still sat slumped at the table. Taliesin's easy assurance was like Rhiann's initial acceptance—incomprehensible. "I can feel your life-force. It's always there for me, calling me. I could take it if I wanted."

"Just as you could kill me with your sword," Taliesin said. "Is it really so different?"

"Do you always end your sentences with questions?" Cade said. "I have no answers for them."

Taliesin leaned forward, resting his hands on the table in front of him. "Yes, you do. This," he waved his hand in front of Cade, indicating both Cade himself and his attitude, "is useless agonizing. Can you become other than what you are?"

"There it is again, another question," Cade said, "but to answer it, no, I can't."

"Then quit your belly-aching. The depredations of your stepfather are only one of the reasons I see for the fall of the Cymry—if not this year, then within the next five—if you do not act. You are your father's heir, the heir to the throne of Arthur. Our enemies hem us in on every side, but of even greater danger is the disunity among the Cymry. Your ride to Powys is only the beginning of the task before you. Only you see what must be done. Only you can unite your people, Cadwaladr. Only you."

"Taliesin—" Cade tried to forestall Taliesin's barrage, but the bard overrode him.

"I didn't make those prophecies to fill the air, you know. I didn't save you from Cadfael so you could feel sorry for yourself. I spoke of you so that when you came, your people would be ready. *He will not die; he will not flee; he will not tire. He will not fade; he will not fail; he will not bend; he will not tremble.* I spoke of you. You must arise!"

"I took Dinas Emrys," Cade said, stung. "I went to Aberffraw."

"And a fine job you made of it," Taliesin said.

"That won't happen again. I learn from my mistakes."

"Good." Taliesin swung his arms, loosening his shoulders. "Because you won't be able to afford many of them."

"Besides," Cade said, "I thought that was why you were here: to keep me out of trouble."

Taliesin laughed, his face transformed from a wizened advisor back to that of a young man. "Ha!" He bowed low before Cade, his arms out, pantomiming a parody of obeisance. "Oh, my most noble and wise lord, I seek only to serve you."

Cade snorted laughter. "Do that again, and I swear I'll choose to become evil after all."

* * * * *

Cade's company of fighters set out from Dinas Emrys less than an hour after midnight. Cade led the men through the gatehouse and down the twisting road that was part of the castle's defenses, to the trail that would take them west to the Roman road. They rode without torches, relying only on Cade's eyes and those of their horses, to guide them.

Rhun and Rhiann followed close behind Cade. They seemed to have come to terms with one another after a rocky start. *I am sorry for the loss of your father,* Cade had heard her say. Rhun had grunted, but now rode at her side. *Progress.*

Cade had felt grief when Rhun's mother, Elen, had died. Everyone had. He'd felt both the horror and the triumph when he'd faced the truth of his new existence, of the power within him. But when he'd ridden into Dinas Emrys with Rhiann at his side, the sole survivor of Cadfael's ambush, and had to look into Rhun's face and tell him that his father and all their men-at-arms were dead, a vast pit of anguish had opened between them.

Although Rhun had embraced Cade and shared his tears with him, Cade didn't know that he'd been able to cross that chasm. Rhun was keeping him at arm's length. Cade feared that through the loss of Cynyr, he'd lose his brother too. He felt so bereft that he'd confessed these fears to Rhiann the following day. She'd suggested that perhaps Rhun felt the same and could express his emotions no more easily than Cade could.

Taliesin was somewhere at the back of the line, even now chanting some song or other that made about as much—or as little—sense as anything else these days: *Cadwaladr opens a way forward in every journey. Woe to the Saxons when they face the Cymry. In the wood, at the plain, on a hill, a candle in the darkness rides with us.*

There it was again. *A candle in the darkness.* Rhiann had quoted that at him too, although from a different refrain.

Goronwy grumbled from his position on Cade's left. "I need a torch." When they'd first started out, several of the newer additions to Cade's company had cursed and lamented the lack of light. Cade had ignored them, knowing they'd either get used to it and accept his leadership, or they wouldn't, and he'd release them from his service. Blindness was one of man's greatest fears. What a man took for granted in the daytime rose up to confound him in the dark.

"It ruins my night vision," Cade said. "In truth, it ruins yours too. Give yourself time, and you'll adjust to the dark."

"I don't know, my lord," Goronwy said. "Some of us were built for the light of day more than others."

"If it makes you feel better," Rhiann said from beside Rhun, "even one torch would broadcast our departure from Dinas Emrys. If my father has men nearby, they would know of it and seek to ambush us or take advantage of our absence to try to take Dinas Emrys back."

Goronwy threw Rhiann an admiring look. "You think like a warrior, lady."

"It must be the clothes." Rhiann laughed. "And maybe the bow."

She was riding comfortably, the reins in her right hand and her bow in her left. On her back, her quiver held a dozen arrows. She seemed to Cade like a goddess of the hunt, perhaps even the *sidhe* goddess, Rhiannon, for whom she was named. He could admit to himself that he didn't want other men like Goronwy finding her desirable. Yet, cursed as he was, he knew that he could never claim a woman as his own, not even one who knew him as well as Rhiann already did.

And he wanted to claim her. The knowledge grew in Cade, and he clenched the hand holding Cadfan's reins. It had been two years since he'd touched anyone beyond a handshake, much less held a woman, for fear of overwhelming them with his power. He'd already touched Rhiann far more than that, and the iron will required not to harm her had done nothing to quell his desire for her. The emptiness that need created did more to feed his fear that he was becoming less than human than anything else possibly could.

Fifty yards farther on, the trail opened onto the fifteen-foot wide highway that was the old Roman road. Cade led the men onto it, and they crowded up behind him.

"We'll ride as quickly as we can," Cade said to Rhun. "Three abreast and in good order."

Rhun nodded. "I'll take up the rear." He raised his voice, relaying Cade's orders to the others. In a moment, Cade found Taliesin on one side of him, and Rhiann on the other. They moved forward in unison, setting a pace that would bring them to the abandoned Roman fort of Tomen-y-mur while it was still dark, and the last few miles to Bryn y Castell by dawn.

"Mother, maiden, crone," Taliesin said.

Cade leaned in closer, uncertain that he'd heard him correctly. "What was that?"

Taliesin shot him a bright glance underneath his bushy eyebrows. "I was musing on the nature of Arianrhod, the goddess who has ensnared you. As mother, she is Modrun, as crone, Cerridwen, and as the maiden, Blodeuwedd, she fell in love with a young lord at Tomen-y-mur. Together, they plotted her husband's death.

Unfortunately for them, he could not be slain except with one foot in bathwater and the other on a goat."

Cade coughed and laughed at the same time. "Why can't I have those conditions? Better than an arrow through the heart or the loss of my head."

Taliesin looked at him, not smiling. "It is no laughing matter."

He was so serious Cade quieted immediately. "You were saying?"

"Every story of Arianrhod offers a window into understanding why she chose you as her champion."

"So I should avoid goats?" Cade said, unable to take the conversation seriously. Taliesin changed so quickly between seriousness and jest that Cade found himself doing the same.

"Cadwaladr," Taliesin said, admonishing him. "The goddess does not act out of whim or spite. Just as there was a reason why I brought you to Bryn y Castell, and a reason why you chose to take Dinas Emrys from Cadfael as your first step toward claiming the throne your father would have left you, there is sense in Arianrhod's actions."

"Agreed." Cade said. "But even you don't know the full meaning behind the prophecies you yourself sing. We are fumbling about in the dark, far more than just on this journey."

"Only some of us are blind now," Taliesin said. "Here, you see clearly. Grant that there are times when you do not, and perhaps another does."

"It's Arianrhod's intentions that interest me," Rhiann said, her words coming slowly as she thought them out. "You called Cade *her champion*. She wants something from Cade, doesn't she? Why else should she transform him? She took the heir to the throne of Gwynedd and made him something far more powerful."

"So I could rule all Wales?" Cade said.

"You'd do that anyway, without her help," Rhiann said. "Besides, is she that interested in the human world and its fleeting needs?"

"No, she isn't," Taliesin said. "Her plans for him address her needs, not his."

Cade shook his head, frustrated as he always was by these thoughts and lack of answers. "It must be something that she cannot do herself."

"Or a task that she doesn't want to be seen doing," Rhiann said. "Until a few days ago, this was all faery talk to me, but the stories speak of the intrigue and back-biting in the world of the *sidhe*, paralleling our own world."

Taliesin smiled and nodded his head, as if he'd already thought of it—which he probably had.

"But what task?" Cade said.

"I don't know," Taliesin said.

Cade stared at him. That Taliesin didn't know—and would actually admit to it—was perhaps the most disconcerting thing of all.

* * * * *

Cade sensed the rising of the sun in the east long before the brightening sky began to obscure the stars. The moon had set several hours before, prompting some grumbling among the men who could see even less than before. Rhiann rode beside Cade throughout the night without complaint, and it occurred to him that very few women would have traveled in this fashion for so long without any protest. He suspected that complaining had never gotten her very far at home and suffering in silence was, for her, normal.

"You have only another hour," Taliesin said.

"And longer still until noon." Cade nodded towards the west. "Those clouds will help."

Rhiann glanced at him. "You foretell the weather too?"

"I would prefer that the sun didn't catch me unawares," Cade said. "It's strength is inversely proportional to my weakness. At least it's February. For me, the summer months are the most difficult to negotiate, when the sun lights the sky for all but a few hours a day, and the least rain falls. That first summer I feigned illness for all of July."

"That can hardly fool the servants for long." Rhiann moved her horse closer to his and lowered her voice so the men behind couldn't hear her.

"No," Cade said. "It can't."

"Does it hurt?" Rhiann said. "The sun?"

"It isn't so much painful as draining," he said. "Such was my problem when I rode to meet your father. I could hold my sword and even maintain my seat on Cadfan, but the sun disoriented me. I can feel my strength ebb as the sun grows higher in the sky."

Rhiann stared at him, clearly fascinated. "How soon after Arianrhod changed you did you discover this?"

Cade wasn't sure how fully he wanted to disclose the intricacies of his affliction to her, but decided to answer anyway. "I knew it the first time the sun hit my face. I fell to the earth, gasping, although I had no breath. There was nothing but blackness before my eyes. Rhun was with me, fortunately, and he dragged me a few feet into the stables.

Even then, we didn't understand that this weakness was part of what Arianrhod had changed in me.

"In the end, Cynyr sent me away from Bryn y Castell. I traveled across Wales under Rhun's protection. Cynyr felt that I needed to learn how I was different from other men, and to deal with what I had become."

"Cadwaladr." Taliesin interrupted him, his voice commanding attention. "A rider comes."

He was looking forward and Cade followed his gaze. A horseman raced towards them out of the gloom, along the straight stretch of road between them and Bryn y Castell. They'd turned northeast from Tomen y Mur a mile back, following the road through a series of hills. Now, the road was heavily treed on either side as it climbed out of the lowlands and farther into the mountains.

Cade checked Cadfan and held up a hand to halt the men. By the time everyone had reined in, the pounding of the oncoming horse's hooves thrummed loudly on the stony road. Cade glanced behind him to catch Rhun's eye and was pleased to see his men shifting into battle formation without needing to be told. Those with spears moved to the front, along with Rhun, who was always at the forefront of any fight.

Rhun pointed with his spear. "Look! More men come behind him!"

He was right. Behind the first rider rode a half-dozen others, obviously in pursuit.

"The first rider must be saved," Taliesin said. "Let him through but hold off the others."

Cade turned to Rhiann. "Take that bow of yours and get off the road. You're not riding in this charge, but if you want to capture that forward rider, I wouldn't mind."

She gave him a steady look and then nodded. "Yes, Cade." She slipped out of line and he turned his attention back to the task at hand. The men were tense and excited. Cade felt the blood lust rising in them—not so different from his own, in truth.

"You too," Cade said to Taliesin. "You need to go with Rhiann."

Taliesin flashed a wicked grin and hefted a spear that had appeared in his hand from out of nowhere. "I'm with you, my boy, come good or ill."

Shaking his head because it was too late to argue with him, and he didn't have the words anyway, Cade spurred Cadfan forward to meet the oncoming men. Ten yards on, the lead rider reached Cade's company, which parted down the center to allow him to flash through the ranks at speed.

Closing the gap again, they neared the opposing force. At their approach, the pursuers visibly hesitated.

"Halt!" The shout came from a helmeted man in the first rank of the approaching company. He threw up his hand, although whether to stop his own men or Cade's wasn't clear. Rhun took the initiative and signaled with his spear for the company to slow. They stopped with fifteen yards left to go between the two forces.

Rhun lifted his chin. "Who are you?"

"That rider is ours!" the man said, not answering Rhun's question. "You must let us through. He belongs to us."

Rhun shifted in his seat and glanced behind him. Cade turned too and saw that Rhiann and the rider in question were now conferring, their heads together. Her bow arm was relaxed at her side, and she'd put her arrow back into her quiver.

"No," Cade said, under his breath, but loud enough for Rhun to hear.

"Who is your lord?" Rhun called to him across the space. Neither company wanted to get any closer.

The man twitched his shoulders, impatient with the delay. "We've tracked the fugitive these many days from Caer Dathyl in Arfon."

Rhun threw Cade a look, knowing, as Cade did, that Cadwallon's kin had held that fort for generations beyond counting.

Cade clicked his tongue to Cadfan and moved in front of his men. "You are speaking to Rhun ap Cynyr of Bryn y Castell, and I am Cadwaladr ap Cadwallon. Tell me the man's crime, and I will see that he is punished."

"My lords!" The man blanched, and his words burst from him in his surprise at who faced him. He looked from Cade to Rhun, who stared impassively back at the captain, giving nothing away.

"He was a serf in our kitchens," the man said. "We were more generous than we should have been with him, and he believed himself better than he is. He stole a horse from our stables and ran away."

"Rides well for a serf, doesn't he?" Rhun said.

While the man sputtered a response, Taliesin spoke in Cade's ear. "The man tells the truth, as far as he knows it. But then, he doesn't know much."

Cade spoke over the man's incoherent stammering. "Tell my uncle, Lord Iaen, that if he will loan the man to me, I'll see to his indenture at Bryn y Castell."

The captain looked away, appearing to study the ditch beside the road before turning back to Cade. "I'm sorry to be the one to tell you, my lord, but your uncle is dead. His eldest son, Teregad, rules in his stead."

"I am very sorry to hear that," Cade said. "How did my uncle die?"

"Old age." The man clipped his words so sharply Cade wondered if that was the whole truth.

Cade kept his voice even. "He lived a good life. His people will miss him."

"So you will return the serf?" the man said, hopefully.

"No," Cade said. "Tell Teregad that the man remains with me."

"King Teregad will not be pleased," the man said.

"You have fulfilled your duty," Rhun said. "You found him. If Teregad seeks further recompense, he may send word to me at Bryn y Castell."

"But he's a thief! Worse than a filthy Saxon!"

"Careful," Cade said. "My mother was born Saxon. You'd be wise to remember it."

"I didn't—" The man broke off and then bowed, knowing he erred and was defeated. "Yes, my lord." Without further protest, he turned his horse around and led his men back up the Roman road. A quarter of a mile on, they exited it onto a track heading west.

"Someone should follow them," Rhun said.

"I share your concern," Cade said. "All is not as it seems."

"We should send Bedwyr," Rhun said.

Cade nodded and signaled to the knight, who rode forward.

"What is my task, my lord?"

"Follow them, but if possible, don't let them see you," Cade said. "That my uncle died so precipitously worries me. I saw him less than three weeks ago after I took Dinas Emrys. At that time, he was in good health. I also don't like it that Teregad sends a half-dozen men to track a kitchen boy."

"You intend that I ride all the way to Caer Dathyl?" Bedwyr said.

"Yes," Cade said. "While I will miss your strength in the upcoming battle, my senses tell me that there is more here than appears on the surface. I'd like you to be my eyes and ears in Caer Dathyl."

"Then you should send me too, my lord."

Cade turned as his cousin, Gwyn, pushed his way to the front of the line. "If something is amiss, Teregad will speak with me as an equal."

Cade studied Gwyn as he sat rigidly on his horse, waiting for acquiescence. Gwyn had appeared at Bryn y Castell fifteen months before, certain that his destiny lay with the true King of Gwynedd, the first of Cade's kin to pledge his loyalty. Cade had accepted Gwyn's allegiance, grateful for it, no less than for Goronwy's, Rhun's, or Bedwyr's—more so, perhaps, because he was kin. "I would prefer that you don't reveal yourself unless it's necessary. I want you both to return safely to Bryn y Castell."

"Yes, my lord," Bedwyr and Gwyn said in unison. Bedwyr slapped Gwyn on the back, and the two men spurred their horses down the road, to disappear along the path the men from Caer Dathyl had taken.

Rhiann and the young escapee were sitting side by side, watching the proceedings. Cade turned Cadfan toward them, but Taliesin sat in his way, contemplating the now empty road in front of him.

"Do you agree?" Cade asked him, not sure if he needed Taliesin's approval, but curious to know what he thought.

"I think so," Taliesin said. "But I had no foresight of this moment and that troubles me."

"Do you usually know everything before it happens?" Cade said, surprised.

Taliesin studied Cade's face. "Up until now, yes."

7

Rhiann

His name was Dafydd. Although he was a large person, with hands like serving platters, from the immaturity in his face, Rhiann didn't think he'd yet reached twenty years of age. Still, he was holding up pretty well for all that. When Rhiann had told him whose company he was now keeping, he'd brightened at the knowledge, while still watching anxiously as Cade covered the twenty yards to where the two of them waited. On his way towards them, Cade again checked the mountains to the east, and then the clouds to the west. By this time, it was light enough to see clearly without a torch, and it didn't look as if the rain was going to come as quickly as Cade had thought.

"Ride and talk," Cade said. "We're two miles from Bryn y Castell. I would hear your story before we reach it."

Dafydd gathered his horse's reins. The animal was breathing more easily, having recovered from his headlong rush along the road. Dafydd urged him forward so he could ride beside Cade.

"Thank you, my lord," Dafydd said. "I feared I faced my death before I'd begun to live."

"Don't take heart yet," Cade said as they returned to the rest of the company. "I haven't decided if I made the right choice. Your pursuer told us you stole your horse. Is that true?"

"No!" Dafydd said, horrified. "Lord Teregad gave it to me; at least I thought he had." He swallowed hard. "Please let me explain. I am Dafydd ap Cynin of Ynys Mana—"

"Brother!" Goronwy had twisted in his seat to look back at Cade and Dafydd, and now swung his horse's head around and stood in his stirrups so he could see them better, a look of complete astonishment on his face. "Sweet Mother of Christ, it's you!"

"Goronwy!" Dafydd's voice went high with excitement.

Goronwy threw himself from his horse and ran back to his brother, who also leapt from his saddle. The brothers met in an enveloping hug. "Young pup!" Goronwy slapped Dafydd on the back. "Last I saw, you were hiding in Mother's skirts as I sailed away."

"Twelve years it's been," Dafydd said. "I set out a year ago from Ynys Manaw to find you, perhaps join you, but my ship was wrecked on the coast of Arfon, and I was taken in at Caer Dathyl."

"Why did you not send word to me at Bryn y Castell that you were here?" Goronwy said.

"At first I didn't know where you were," Dafydd said, "and then I was not in a position to do so."

"But you must have told them who you were!" Goronwy said.

Dafydd looked sheepish. "I was ashamed to have arrived on the shore with no possessions—no horse, sword or armor. I asked King Iaen if I could work in his kitchen for a year. At the end of that year, if I'd proved my worth, I would tell him my name, and he might give me a horse and sword."

"His kitchens!" Goronwy said. "That is no place for the son of the king of Ynys Manaw!"

"I learned about myself, there," Dafydd said, his voice quiet but firm. "At home, I was a pampered prince. At Caer Dathyl, I worked with and among the common people. Their lot was mine. Once I began, I felt a need to persevere, to prove to myself that I could be both prince and pauper if I had to."

"What changed?" Cade said. "Obviously, you felt you could no longer stay at Caer Dathyl, or you wouldn't be here now."

"My year was up," Dafydd said. "I am the son of a king, and my responsibilities are, in the end, the greater for it. But Lord Iaen died before I could tell him who I was. Instead, I confessed the truth to Teregad, his eldest son and heir. He swore to honor his father's agreement, but he kept putting off the day. Finally, four days ago, I pressed him hard, and he gave me the horse and sword that Lord Iaen had promised me. I rode away."

"And he sent men out to reclaim what you'd taken," Cade said, "never telling them your true name."

Dafydd shrugged. "It appears so, my lord."

"I've seen Teregad at Aberffraw," Rhiann said. "He's eaten at my father's table many times."

Cade turned to her. "That is not welcome news." Then he glanced at the mountains to the east again, for perhaps the twentieth time since the conversation began.

"My lord—" Goronwy said.

Cade held up his hand. "We will speak more and outfit your brother properly once we reach Bryn y Castell. Now, I must ride!"

He kicked Cadfan into a gallop. Within a heartbeat, Cade was ten lengths ahead of the rest of his company. Rhiann glanced at the tip of the mountain to the east, fearing that the sun was already shining above it. There was a small cloud there, filtering the light, but around it was blue sky.

"Why—" Dafydd said.

Goronwy growled and urged his horse to follow. "Never mind." Soon everyone was riding hard. The company streamed out in a long line behind Cade, racing the rising sun.

A galloping horse can travel thirty miles in an hour, but can't move that quickly for very long. Cade's horse flew up the road to Bryn y Castell faster than Rhiann would have thought possible.

Initially, they'd been riding east, such that when the sun topped the peak, it would have shone full onto Cade's face. Before that could happen, Cade turned north along the path to the fort that led from the Roman road, which they'd followed all the way from Dinas Emrys. Cade slowed to traverse the steep trail just as the sun burst through the cloud. Cade slumped forward—and then his horse carried him through the gatehouse and into the fort.

Rhun cursed as he galloped past Rhiann, racing ahead of the others. "Damn Arianrhod to the deepest, darkest recesses of Annwn."

By the time Rhiann trotted her horse into the courtyard of the fort, Rhun had Cade off Cadfan. Cade wove a little on his feet, but was otherwise upright, safe for now in the shadow of the gatehouse.

"This must stop, my lord," Rhun said. "You cannot continue this way."

"And yet," Taliesin said from beside Rhiann, calmly straightening his robes after dismounting, "we have arrived in good order, safe, and having rescued Goronwy's brother from his pursuers. All in all, there have been few nights in my experience that have been quite this successful."

It hadn't occurred to Rhiann to look at it that way.

On the inside, Bryn y Castell was much like Aberffraw. It had a high fence which surrounded the wooden hall and provided plenty of room for stables, craft houses, and living quarters for Rhun's people. On the outside, however, it was very different, and she relished that difference. The fort sat upon a hilltop overlooking the valley they'd come up from Tomen y Mur and was otherwise ringed by mountains. In the distance, she could see the sea, a blue-gray smudge in the morning sun.

Cade stood in deep shadow inside the doorway to the guardroom. "You and Rhiann need rest," he told Rhun. "Could you find her a place to sleep? I'd like to speak with Taliesin alone. You and I can talk again before we ride tonight."

Rhun's face went blank, as if he was holding back something he wanted to say but felt he couldn't, at least not with others listening. Instead, he turned to Rhiann. In the small space, he towered over her, but she no longer found him intimidating. He was concerned for Cade, and she respected that.

"Come," Rhun said. The two of them started across the courtyard to the hall in silence. After three strides, Rhiann decided she needed to break it.

"I know there's little you wouldn't do for him," she said, by way of a beginning. Between the two of them, there was no need to clarify who *him* was. Rhiann walked another pace before she realized Rhun had stopped.

"Why are you here?" he said. "It makes no sense to me."

"Why are you?" Rhiann said.

"Because all my life I've followed Cade," Rhun said, surprising Rhiann with the simple truth. "I can't imagine doing anything different now, just because he's no longer human."

"He is human," Rhiann said, "just something more than human too."

Rhun had begun shaking his head at her words before she'd finished speaking. "No. Cade walks among us, but he died in that cave, just as in the stories. Surely you've heard them? *Bran, the mighty and terrible, towered over the land of the Cymry, a scourge upon his enemies; until the day she called him, her song beckoning him from across the hills. Into her arms he fell, his soul consumed, a mighty man undone.*"

"I know it," Rhiann said. "And I suppose I even believe it now. Yet, why isn't Cade a demon like all the others?"

Rhun froze. "Others?" He stepped forward and took her by the shoulders. "What others?"

"Other ... creatures." Rhiann paused as she searched for the words. "Cade killed a man who wasn't a man right in front of me the other night, before we arrived in Dinas Emrys. He didn't tell you?"

"You're sure the man was a demon?" Rhun said.

"His face transformed into a mask like I've never seen on any man," Rhiann said. "Apparently, Cade has killed many such beings. He says there are more like Madoc and worse as well that he refuses to describe to me."

"By the goddess, so that's what he's been doing every night," Rhun breathed. "All this time I've been worried about him, not knowing where he goes and what he does."

"What do you mean?" Rhiann said.

Rhun was still shaking his head. "Cade wanders at night. I've not known why. I thought he was too ashamed to tell me. Instead, it must be that he felt it would be boasting."

"You were afraid he was killing humans," Rhiann said, her understanding growing. "Despite everything you know of him, you feared he'd lost control of his power."

"The *sidhe* and their victims were a faery story until Cade came back from that cave. He was cold and clammy—and terrified to find himself without breath or heartbeat. It was only later we discovered the dark light within him that takes all his will to contain." Rhun shook his head again. "All I can tell you is that despite all that, he is still the Cade I love."

"Cade the *sidhe* scares me," Rhiann said. "I can see the power inside him sometimes when I look at him in a certain way, or catch his eye from a certain angle."

Rhun focused on her face. "You are the daughter of a king. I ask again: why you are here? Look at you, dressed as a boy, with no possessions save that which Cade chooses to give you."

"He gave me his word," Rhiann said. "Isn't that enough?"

Rhun nodded his head slowly. "Yes. It's always been enough for me too."

They studied each other for a count of five, and then Rhun held out his arm to her. Rhiann took it. He escorted her up the steps and through a massive door that opened onto the great hall. The hall itself was unusual in that it was as wide as it was deep. Once inside, the bright sunlight was extinguished because the hall had no windows. Looking more closely, Rhiann could see the places where it once had had them, but they'd been blocked, undoubtedly for Cade's sake.

Servants—slaves probably, though none wore the collar—were busy laying out a meal. A young woman stood near a door set in the opposite wall, and at the sight of Rhiann and Rhun, came forward, walking straight into Rhun's arms.

"I'm so sorry, Rhun." The woman hugged him, her cheek pressed to his chest. "The rider arrived a few days ago with your message. There is much grief here."

Rhun kissed the top of the woman's head. "I know, Bronwen. In my heart too."

Rhun turned to Rhiann. "Rhiann, I'd like you to meet Bronwen, my wife and the mother of my son, Cador. Bronwen, please welcome Rhiannon, of Aberffraw."

"Aberffraw!" Bronwen looked Rhiann up and down, taking in her masculine clothing, quiver, and bow.

"Rhiann helped Cade to escape from Cadfael." Rhun paused, and Rhiann wondered if he was debating whether or not he should mention that Cadfael was Rhiann's father. Instead, he said. "If not for her, Cade would be dead along with all the others."

Bronwen took Rhiann's hand. "Thank you, Rhiann. You are welcome at Bryn y Castell." She gestured with one hand toward the head table, where Goronwy and Dafydd were already sitting. Rhiann and Rhun walked to it and found seats across from them. The two men were discussing Cade.

"Is he ill?" Dafydd speared a parsnip with his belt knife and chewed it. Goronwy, Rhun, and Rhiann exchanged glances, but before any of them could speak, Dafydd went on talking. "Because looking at his symptoms, he looks a lot like our great uncle Dane." Dafydd waved his knife at Goronwy. "You remember? Late in life he started to have a hard time with bright sun—"

"Dafydd," Goronwy said. "That's not it."

"How do you know?" Dafydd said. "It started in his eyes and then his weakness began to effect his ability to keep his seat on a horse. Do you remember when he fell off his horse into the pig—"

Dafydd!" Goronwy said again. "Shut up."

Dafydd closed his mouth on the words he'd been about to speak.

Goronwy took in a breath and let it out. "Uncle Dane had syphilis. Lord Cadwaladr has been touched by the gods."

Rhun growled. "Touched is right."

"What do you mean?" Dafydd looked confused. "What do you mean by *touched*?"

"He has become of the *sidhe*, with the power to take a man's life merely by touching him." Rhiann patted one of Dafydd's enormous hands that he'd laid flat on the table. His food and drink were forgotten. "Despite this, you need not worry. Lord Cadwaladr is not going to hurt you."

"Well of course not!" Dafydd said. "He's the Pendragon, isn't he? Taliesin foresaw that his name would be remembered with Arthur's among the Cymry for as long as our land endures. I can't believe I'm actually sitting at the same table where he has sat." Dafydd looked around. "Does everybody else know?"

"Some do," Rhun said. "Those we trust. We prefer not to talk about it. We let visitors and the talkative draw their own conclusions."

"I understand." Dafydd nodded. "We wouldn't want it bandied about that the heir to the throne of the High King steals the life-force of other men. What would the common folk say?"

"That's not exactly it, Dafydd," Rhiann said. "Cade himself would rather we treated him normally."

"Normally for the heir to the throne of Gwynedd, anyway," Goronwy said. Rhun and Rhiann nodded, while Dafydd looked from one to the other. Then he started to smile.

"It's all right," he said. "I get it. This is a jest, right? You're having fun with me, the little brother."

The three others gazed steadily at him. It was Rhun who shook his head. "No."

Dafydd opened his mouth to say something, closed it, and then opened it again. He sat, slack-jawed, until Goronwy reached across the table to push up his chin. Instantly, Dafydd leaned forward and spoke in a loud whisper. "There is more to this story. You must tell me!" His bright eyes were alight with interest.

"The goddess Arianrhod lured Lord Cadwaladr into a cave and kissed him. In doing so, she changed him into the being he is now, but leaving him still in this world," Rhun said. "He is *sidhe*, yet walks among us."

"Why?" Dafydd said. "What does she want from him?" He kept going, answering his own question. "For want something she must. Like with Lord Pwyll when Arawn befriended him, for every encounter with the gods, there is a price to pay."

"We don't know what she wants," Goronwy said.

"Well, it could be anything, couldn't it?" Dafydd rubbed his chin as he mused. "Maybe she just liked him or—"

"She told him that she'd been waiting for him for a long time," Rhiann said. "She kissed him and left him and he hasn't seen her since."

"So is he immortal too? Has he truly become a god?" Dafydd said, his mind skipping from one idea to the next.

"He believes he can die as any other demon—an arrow through his heart or by the loss of his head," Goronwy said. "Otherwise, if it is true that he has no soul, then yes, he is immortal."

"That's incredible!" Then Dafydd sobered. "Is he going to kill you for telling me?" He shifted in his seat. "Or me?"

"No," Rhun said, shortly. And then a devilish twinkle appeared in his eye. "Or rather, I don't think so."

Dafydd's eyes widened. For the amount of time it took for everyone to take a deep breath, Goronwy, Rhun, and Rhiann studied Dafydd, who'd become uncharacteristically silent, even if his brain was spinning with ideas.

"It just occurred to me that while Lord Cadwaladr is the first *sidhe* I have encountered, he's not the first, uh—," Dafydd paused, searching for the proper word as Rhiann had earlier, "—soulless creature I have come upon, although I didn't realize it until just now."

Rhun threw up his hands. "Why has everyone encountered one but me? Where did you see him?"

"At Caer Dathyl," Dafydd said. "I sat next to him at dinner one day."

"If he ate dinner," Goronwy said, "he wouldn't be a demon."

"Cade can eat," Rhun said. "He just doesn't need to, and it tastes like sawdust in his mouth."

Goronwy nodded. "Granted," he said, and then to Dafydd. "Go on."

"I didn't think anything of him at first—not until it occurred to me that he was well-dressed and wore fine armor, and yet was sitting with the servants. He ate very little and brought his own flask. He poured the contents into his cup, which he didn't share."

"None of which makes him a demon," Goronwy said.

"How about that he didn't breathe?" Dafydd said.

"That would do it," Rhun said.

"Did you notice at the time that he didn't breathe?" Rhiann said.

"Yes," Dafydd said. "I did, except I didn't, if you know what I mean."

"No, we don't," Goronwy said.

"Yes, we do." Rhiann glared at Goronwy, who was just being a difficult older brother. "Often you notice things that you don't become fully conscious of until something strikes you as similar. Is that right, Dafydd?"

Dafydd nodded. "It was the way he drank, actually, that got my attention. He tipped up his cup and just ... drank. He swallowed and swallowed and never had to take a breath. And when he was done his eyes were red."

That prompted another glance between Rhun and Goronwy. "Cade's eyes turn a glowing green when he becomes a *sidhe*," Rhun said.

"Madoc's were red too," Rhiann said.

"Who's Madoc?" Goronwy and Dafydd asked together.

Rhiann sighed, not wanting to relive it all again but knowing she was going to have to satisfy their curiosity. So she told them.

8

Cade

Cade licked his lips and swallowed hard. The fort vibrated with life, flooding his senses to the point where he was having a hard time damping it down. He'd sent Taliesin away—as he always sent everyone away—not so much afraid that he couldn't control himself, but because he didn't want Taliesin to see him struggle. In addition, wizard or not, like the others Taliesin needed to sleep.

That first awful evening after Arianrhod had changed him, Cade had regained consciousness in the cave. He'd been alone, but with a heat burning in him that grew to a fire that threatened to consume him. Barely conscious of his actions, he'd chased and caught a rabbit with his bare hands, stunning himself with the speed of his movements. When he discovered that as he touched it, it died, he'd thrown it away in panic. Worse, the creature's death had eased the pain within him.

He'd staggered back down the mountain through the snow, able to see easily and untouched by the cold in the air around him. He'd led Cadfan instead of riding him, and it was only the small sense of himself that remained within him that prevented him from killing his horse too. He'd returned to Bryn y Castell, finding his way without difficulty, until he'd reached the still-open gates to the fort. The guards had been about to close them on the night when Cade had attempted to walk through them.

Instead, he had come to a halt, butting up against an unseen barrier. As was the case with the gods themselves, he couldn't enter a human home uninvited. Arianrhod had known that; it was why she had waited for him in a cave, rather than trap him in his own room. The guard had looked at Cade curiously, not understanding why he hadn't walked inside. Then the guard had broken the spell by welcoming Cade inside the gates with a word and a gesture.

The guard had been relieved to see him, since Cade had been gone so long, but Cade's inability to enter his own home uninvited shocked him, perhaps even more than what had happened with the rabbit. Cade had stumbled into the courtyard and released Cadfan to a stable boy who'd run to take him. Then the fire had overcome him again, stoked by the press of humanity in the fort.

He strode into the hall, blind to everything but the need within him. Many men remained at the tables, having finished the evening meal, but what had caught Cade's attention was a servant, just entering the kitchen at the rear of the hall. He went after her. As he grabbed her, the power coursed through him. At the same instant, that part of him that remembered that he was Cade, a human being, recoiled. *What are you doing?* he'd shouted to himself. *Are you so much an animal that you would kill an innocent girl?*

When Cade clenched his fingers around her arms, the girl had screamed. With a force of will he hadn't ever before needed, Cade regained some measure of control. He pushed the girl away. She fell, and Cade collapsed to his knees.

Cynyr and Rhun had found him then. The girl was unconscious but alive—and Cade was dead. That first evening, not truly realizing what was wrong with him but horrified beyond measure and thinking they'd a viper in their midst, they'd thrown Cade into a cell at the back of the stables. Unfortunately for a murderer they'd been keeping there, Cade's control of his power remained tenuous. The man had been destined for the gallows. Cade had killed him instead.

Cynyr and Rhun had been afraid of Cade, but no more than he'd been afraid of himself. He'd huddled in the corner with the dead body, sobbing, full of loathing at what he'd become. He'd begged his family to kill him. Instead, they'd shown mercy. That second evening of Cade's new life, Rhun brought him a chicken destined for the stewpot. Cade had wrung its life-force from it. Afterwards, Cynyr had unlocked his prison door and hunkered down in front of Cade.

"Are you going to kill me?" Cynyr had said.

Cade had shaken his head, nearly frantic with pain and horror. "No, no, no."

"Then you must learn how to live with this," Cynyr had said. "You must never find yourself so consumed by need that you become what you cannot be."

So Cade had done as his foster father had asked. Over time, he'd learned to judge the extent of his weakness and to isolate himself until the worst of the longing passed. He no longer needed to kill animals to control his power—they'd only ever been a temporary and ineffective half-measure anyway. Instead, he'd learned control.

Not that he hadn't learned how to kill men, quickly and efficiently, and how to use the strength the killing gave him. Taliesin had mocked the priests when he'd pointed out that if all people were fundamentally evil, there was no difference between them and Cade. But Cade knew that Taliesin was wrong.

A knock came at the door, and Cade pushed away from the wall. "Come in."

The door creaked open, revealing Rhiann, silhouetted in the doorway by the daylight behind her, the promised rainclouds having moved to the north. She was so vibrant, Cade could feel her life-force rolling over him and wanted it—wanted her. The darkness rose within him, and he clenched his hands into fists to push the power back down. Closing his eyes, he backed away, deeper into the darkened corner of the room that he couldn't help but make less dark. His appearance had scared her when he'd killed the Saxon archer. His countenance would frighten her now. *And maybe I need it to.*

"Cade?" Rhiann hesitated on the threshold, peering through the gloom for him.

"I'm here, Rhiann." Cade opened his eyes, hoping that he'd tamed himself enough that they no longer glowed.

"Oh." Her eyes fastened on his and widened.

"Leave, Rhiann."

"I don't mind being with you. It isn't that I don't care what you are, but that I would know it all, if you will share it."

"I mind," he said.

She didn't move. "We told Dafydd. He wants to stay and serve you."

Cade stayed in his corner. Rhiann wasn't leaving and her refusal forced him to change tactics. He trained his full attention on her, releasing just a bit of the power within him in order to glare at her across the space that separated them. Even he could see the light that caused his outline to subtlety shimmer.

Rhiann still didn't take the hint. "Cade." Her face was very pale, and her hand was to her throat, but she still didn't run from him as he'd expected and hoped. *No, not hoped.*

A growl formed in his throat. "You need to leave me, Rhiann."

"Why?" she said. "Help me to understand."

I spin around so quickly she doesn't even have time to flinch before I have her up against the far wall of the guardroom. "This is why." My mouth comes down on hers, and I tighten my arms around her. She doesn't struggle or cry, just holds still as I pull her closer, wanting to scare her away from me, but yet not wanting to. As I deepen the kiss, I realize I've failed utterly. She relaxes into me and snakes her arms around my neck.

Heaven help me, I'm lost.

I finally release her and ease back, searching her face for a response beyond what she's already given me. She is a little wide-eyed, her lips puffy, unaccustomed to the attention I've given them. She reaches up and rubs the side of my jaw with her hand.

"Did you think that would drive me away?"

"It was my intent," I admit.

"It's not going to work."

Cade pressed one palm to the wall and rubbed his forehead with the other, shaking off the vision and shocked that he'd allowed it to come to the forefront of his mind. The self-control required to both kiss her and keep her alive was beyond him. He knew that. "Rhiann. I can't ... I'm not ..." Helpless and near tears, Cade was at a loss for how to continue. He pressed his forehead to the wall, feeling the coolness of the stone, and closed his eyes. "Just go."

Cade's anger hadn't moved her, but his obvious grief—grief that he wouldn't share with her—caused her to turn away. In a rush, Rhiann reached behind her, threw open the door, and fled. Her footsteps pounded away across the courtyard to the keep. It was what he wanted, except it wasn't, and he knew he wasn't going to be able to return to the shadows in peace.

For a time after Rhiann left, Cade tortured himself with visions of her in another man's arms—a knight such as Goronwy, or heaven help him, young Dafydd. More frustrated than ever, he paced around the small space, growing more and more angry until his eyes began to glow again and bursts of light flashed from his fingertips. That brought him up short. Taliesin had reminded him that he had a job to do. What was important was the unity of Wales. What was important was the defeat of the Saxons and the demons arising from the Underworld. What was not important was his own, personal happiness.

Still restless, Cade walked out of the guardroom and stood underneath the gatehouse, watching more clouds come in from the southwest. They were late, but as this was Wales, they always came eventually. Below him, the crag of Garreglwyd rose hundreds of feet above the fort. Farther south lay Hyrddod and Rhobell Fawr. And then south of Llyn Tegin, the mountains continued: Hen Gerrig, Aran Fawddwy, Bryn Amlwg. Tonight, they would ride around them to the east before they met the Saxons. Fortunately, the Romans were pragmatists and knew as well as anyone that when faced with a mountain, it was better to go around it than over it. There was no quicker way to get across Wales than to follow the roads they'd built. Cade and his men had a long ride ahead of them tonight, and probably the night after that.

Because of his vantage point on southwestern slope, Cade was able to watch the rain cross the valley, the clouds flying before the wind, before it hit Bryn y Castell. The sky was dark enough to protect him now, but he wanted to wait for the rain before he crossed the courtyard to the hall. The feast couldn't begin until he did, and he chided himself for not standing beside Rhun earlier. And yet, he was dreading this evening and stayed still.

The feast would not be one of victory, nor celebration, but to mark the ascension of Rhun to his father's place. Cade had watched Rhun's vassals arriving at Bryn y Castell all day. Soon they would pledge their allegiance to him as his father's son. In truth, it hurt Cade that Rhun had accepted his condolences at his father's death, but hadn't acknowledged that Cynyr had been Cade's father too, even if they didn't share a blood tie. Cade missed Cynyr, missed his bellowing call as he entered his own hall. Now there was only Rhun, bowed by the burden of his new responsibilities, both to his father, and without a doubt, to Cade.

Within the hour, rain began to pit-patter on the stones in front of the gate, and then on the gatehouse itself. Cade stepped forward, out of the fort, until he stood clear of the roof. He closed his eyes and tipped his face upwards, feeling the staccato of rain on his face and reveling in his ability to stand in the daylight without fear. Cade opened his eyes. Black clouds covered the sky from one end of the valley to the other. It was going to be a wet and miserable night of riding. And hopefully, a wet and miserable day tomorrow.

Cade strode into the great hall, head high, feeling restored. And then he saw the look on Rhun's face, and his step faltered. He'd gotten lost in his thoughts of the rain and the waning of the day and forgotten—only just for a moment but it was enough—that Cynyr was dead. The weight of the loss sagged Cade's shoulders again. Chastened, he made his way around the edge of the room to where Rhun sat near the fire, watching his people assemble.

Cade came to a halt at Rhun's side, putting out a hand to rest it on his shoulder, and then pulling it back before he touched him. "I'm sorry. If I could take it all back, I would. If I hadn't been chasing a foolish dream, Father would still be alive."

Rhun leaned forward to stare deeper into the flames, his chin in his hands. "My father's death was not your fault, Cade. I would have gone to Anglesey too, had you let me, and that hurts more than anything. Perhaps I could have saved him; saved all of them."

Cade walked to the mantle and leaned against it, his forehead pressing against the back of his hand. "Cynyr came to Anglesey for me. Even if I'd had my full strength, we could not have won out. Cadfael's men outnumbered us four to one. I should not have reached for the throne of Gwynedd."

At that, Rhun's face took on the look of a storm. He surged to his feet, bringing his nose to within inches of Cade's. "You damn well better not give up, Cade! This is not just about you anymore."

Cade stood his ground. "Do I have a choice, Rhun? Look at me! I am a danger to myself and everyone around me. The crown of the High King is as easily yours as mine. You are descended from great kings as much as I."

Rhun was shaking his head back and forth like an angry bull. "No, Cade. I will not hear your excuses. It is you who are Arthur's heir; you of whom the prophecies speak; you and no other. Don't you dare walk away from this."

Cade was taken aback at Rhun's vehemence, for he so rarely lost his temper. Accepting that appeasement was the only answer in this moment, despite his doubts, Cade nodded. "Taliesin said as much to me yesterday. With your support, I will see that the dragon standard is raised above every castle in Gwynedd."

The room had filled as they talked. It was late afternoon by now, and the smell of roasting pig wafted through the hall. Taliesin appeared beside Rhun and put a hand on his shoulder. "It is time. If we are to leave as the sun sets, we must begin the ceremony."

Rhun walked to the edge of the dais that held the high table. Turning to face the entrance to the hall, he held up his hands for silence. Instantly, the men, women, and children, who'd come from the surrounding countryside on such short notice to see him, quieted.

"My father and many of your loved ones met their deaths at the hand of Cadfael of Gwynedd," he began, deliberately not according Cadfael the title of *king*. "They are all at peace, now, in the land across the Strait. Even so, they are with us today, just as my father, Cynyr, is in me, and in my foster brother, Cadwaladr, at whose side he rode."

At his words, Cade's throat closed over tears that he could no longer shed. Rhun then opened his arms wide, welcoming his people to offer him their allegiance. With a scrape of benches and a low murmur of voices, they came forward one by one, in pairs, or in family groups. Cade moved to within arm's length of Rhun, standing close enough throughout the ceremony to offer support, but far enough away that it was clear that Rhun was the Lord of Bryn y Castell, not Cade.

Nearly one hundred souls pledged their lives to Rhun. Afterwards, they gathered at the tables for the feast, toasting the new lord of Bryn y Castell. Rhun sat heavily in the central position in his father's chair and accepted their accolades, if reluctantly.

"He loves them all." Rhiann had stood by the fire for the ceremony, and now Cade joined her there. Her eyes were clearer, even as she rubbed the last of the sleep from them.

It surprised Cade that she was still willing to talk to him, but he felt it only civil to answer her. "They've learned over the years as he sat beside his father that he was fair. They give him their loyalty willingly, and with the knowledge that he will die for them sooner than they would die for him."

"My father wouldn't die for anyone," Rhiann said.

Cade glanced at her. "No. I imagine he wouldn't."

The feast wasn't even half over before Taliesin was at Cade's side again. "We must go."

A man-at-arms disappeared through the entrance to the hall, and Cade checked the sky that showed briefly before the door closed. The sun was down, although it was not quite dark. "I would've liked to have been gone by now. But this is Rhun's hour, and he needs to see it through."

Taliesin shook his head. "No. Time is short."

Cade focused on Taliesin more closely. "What do you *see*?"

"A great wave," Taliesin said. "It is reaching the shore and will soon flood the beach. We may not even be in time to stop it if we were to leave this instant, but I only know that we must try."

"Tell Rhun of your vision," Cade said. "I could order him to leave, but I would rather it was his decision today."

Taliesin nodded and made his way to the head table where Rhun sat holding court. Cade turned to Rhiann. "You still insist that you ride with us?"

"With you," she said. "Even more so than before."

"I am loath to put you in danger," Cade said.

"I don't care for the thought either," Rhiann said, "but Taliesin told me that I had to come; that my role could be as vital as anyone's."

"We'll have at least thirty men, many of whom are not as familiar with me as those who rode from Dinas Emrys. Many come from surrounding estates and have spent little time at Bryn y Castell. You must remain either with Rhun, Taliesin, or me at all times."

"Not all these men know the truth of you, do they?" she said.

"They all know," Cade said. "Not all believe. It is likely, however, that they all will know me before the night is out."

"They will accept you," she said.

"Not all of them." Cade couldn't read Rhiann's expression, but thought to remind her of what had happened in the guardroom, in case the image was fading faster than it should. "I'm not human, Rhiann."

"I'm not so sure of that, despite what you and Rhun say." She didn't look at Cade as she spoke, instead watching Taliesin converse with Rhun.

"I can't spend time with you," Cade said. "I can't be with you or any woman. You can't want it."

"You have held yourself aloof from other people," Rhiann said. "That is no way to live."

"I'm not alive! I stay away from people out of courtesy and fear!" He swung around and made to drive his fist into the wall. It would call attention to himself, however, which he didn't want, and he arrested the movement at the last moment before spinning back to her. "Do you not realize what you do to me? How dangerous I could be to you?" He pressed her harder. "I spoke to Taliesin yesterday about what was inside me—both good and evil. Today I feel the evil welling up within me."

Cade held her eyes, which had widened, much like he'd imagined in his vision, but he knew that it had to be out of fear, not love. Then, Cade looked over at Taliesin, who'd finished his consultation with Rhun.

Rhun stood, nodded, and signaled to the men in the company that the time had come to leave. He raised his voice above the crowd. "I have word that Lord Geraint has need of our spears in the south. The men who will ride with Lord Cadwaladr must come now."

The people in the hall initially hushed at his words, and then the murmuring grew loud again as Rhun strode toward the double doors leading out of the hall. Ready to get moving and put his restless energy to good use, Cade followed.

The Last Pendragon Saga continues with the second novella in the series: *The Pendragon's Blade*

Printed in Great Britain
by Amazon

56882541R00093